'I've carefully built myself a life, and it's a good life. I'm a doctor and I intend to become a damn good one. I'm on my own, and I intend to stay that way.' She glared defiantly across to Andrew.

'And along comes Andrew McIntyre, disturbing your careful plans.'

'You're not disturbing me at all,' she assured him.

'Alex, you have this nasty habit of telling fibs!'

She glared at him.

'Alex,' his voice was infinitely gentle, 'I won't hurt you.'

DARE TO
LOVE AGAIN

BY
MARION LENNOX

MILLS & BOON LIMITED
ETON HOUSE   18-24 PARADISE ROAD
RICHMOND   SURREY   TW9 1SR

*First published in Great Britain 1990
by Mills & Boon Limited*

© Marion Lennox 1990

*Australian copyright 1990
Philippine copyright 1990
This edition 1990*

ISBN 0 263 76794 9

*Set in Times 10 on 12 pt.
03 – 9004 – 57492*

Typeset in Great Britain by The Picador Group, Bristol

Made and Printed in Great Britain

CHAPTER ONE

TO BOARD the aircraft had taken more courage than Alex knew she possessed. As the plane reached its cruising height the occupants of the cabin relaxed. Those used to the flight across Tasmania's rugged west opened magazines or settled down for a chat, while newcomers to the flight gazed appreciatively down at the mountainous country beneath them. Alex released her breath and unclenched her hands. They hurt. She opened her eyes to see blood welling through broken skin where her nails had bitten into her palms, and shakily she started to search in her bag for a tissue. A large red handkerchief appeared across the arm rest between herself and her neighbour.

For the first time she became aware of the occupant of the seat beside her. He was a small, rotund man in his fifties, his face a mixture of sympathy and interest. Alex gave him a wavery smile and returned the handkerchief as she located her own. Sympathy was one thing she could do without.

Her neighbour, had she known it, was eyeing her with considerably more than sympathy. Six years ago, when Alex was twenty-two, Chris had referred to her as a stunner. Six years of maturity had only added to her magnificent looks. She was tall and willow-slim. Her deep chestnut hair curled in wisps, framing a pale face which seemed almost too small to hold the huge dark eyes. The dark shadows, a legacy from six years before, were partly masked by make-up but showed through enough to give her almost an ethereal appearance. A lovely face, mused the man beside her, a serene, gentle face.

Alex was feeling anything but serene. The flight which she had schooled herself for so long to take was calling for all her stock of self-control. She kept her eyes firmly away from the windows, fixed on the seat in front of her, but still her fingers clenched relentlessly. This was crazy! Once, flying had been so easy.

Against her will her mind went back to that last flight, her last time with Chris and Timmy. The glorious sunshine and the view, miles and miles of open country stretching away as far as they could see beneath the plane. Herds of wild horses, brumbies, wheeling away in fright as they passed overhead. Isolated stations with tiny doll-like figures waving up at them. The feeling of pure happiness within the cramped cockpit as Chris's eyes met hers over Timmy's sleepy head. Then the nightmare, the moments that would never go away. The sudden splutter and lurch of engine failure. Chris's eyes, filled with panic. His voice over the radio, calm despite his eyes, giving the world their position. The slow spiral, the feel of Timmy's fingers clutched around hers. Then darkness.

Alex came back to reality to realise someone was shaking her arm.

'Excuse me, are you all right? Would you like me to call the hostess?'

She focused on her neighbour's face, bent close towards her with concern. The darkness receded, and with an effort she pulled herself together. She was making an absolute fool of herself! She'd obviously shaken her neighbour badly.

'I'm so sorry. I must have really let myself go.' She gave him a rueful grin and tried to divert the conversation. 'You never get frightened in these things yourself?'

He gave an almost audible sigh of relief, and Alex found she could relax enough to grin. Obviously the thought of a hysterical travelling companion horrified the poor man.

'Thank God for that, then!' He peered at her again, his anxiety not wholly allayed. 'Promise you won't faint? To be quite honest, I shouldn't have a clue what to do. Scream myself, most likely.' He proffered a barley sugar which Alex accepted gratefully. 'Where are you heading?'

'Pirrengurra.'

He almost fell off his seat.

'Pirrengurra! Nobody goes to Pirrengurra.'

'I do.' Alex's reply was defensive.

He laughed and went on apologetically.

'I'm sorry—don't jump on me like that. As a matter of fact, I'm going there myself. I'm an auditor and am supposed to spring a surprise visit every six months or so just to keep the local bank on its toes, although,' he went on reflectively, 'how I'm supposed to make it a surprise when there's only one flight in a week, one taxi to meet the plane and one pub to book into when you get there I don't know. I always book using a false name, but every time I've walked into the bank they've greeted me by my alias. They take pride in it.'

Alex smiled, and some of the tension ebbed away as they introduced each other.

Charlie Taylor's curiosity was at war with his good manners, and it finally got the better of him.

'Why on earth are you going to Pirrengurra? Do you know it?' As Alex shook her head he continued, 'It would have to be one of the wildest, most remote logging communities in the west of Tasmania. It's magnificent country if you like scenery, but personally,' he shuddered, 'I like staying at home looking at photographs on the calendar. Are you staying long?'

Alex put him out of his misery. 'I hope so. I'm a doctor

and I'm taking a job as an assistant. I gather the local doctor is badly overworked.'

Charlie whistled in surprise and his eyes once again swept her appreciatively.

'You are some package, lady!' he declared.

It was impossible to be offended with Charlie; he exuded warmth and good spirit. The terrors of the flight receded as Alex settled back to enjoy his gossip.

And gossip it was. Charlie, for one who visited the place once every six months, seemed to know everyone in the town.

'You'll be working for Andrew McIntyre.' He eyed her speculatively. 'I honestly don't know how he's going to take to you. He's got a reputation as being a hard man to work with, and the last lady doctor who tried the place out only lasted a week. Rumour has it she cried from Pirrengurra to Hobart.'

Interested in spite of herself, Alex couldn't help asking, 'Why? Do you know?'

'Well,' Charlie was enjoying himself, 'it's said he just doesn't like women, although I must admit the opposite doesn't seem to be true. The nursing staff seem to think a bit of him, and the matron is said to have her eyes fixed fairly firmly on him as a matrimonial prospect. He'd be better off out of that, though.' He paused reflectively. 'A cold piece of work if ever I met one.'

This conversation was most improper. Reluctantly Alex steered the conversation on to less personal matters. What was the town like? What were the people like?

She knew a little—the job advertisement had given the bare outlines. The description had skated over what made it for Alex the most desirable of all the positions she had considered: it was remote and she knew nobody. She'd had enough sympathy to last a lifetime and was desperate to be treated with indifference once again.

Alex had been two years into her medical course when she met Chris, a pilot with an airline serving the remote north of Australia. Afterwards—well, it seemed the only thing left, to take up the threads of medicine. This job was as far away from Australia's burning North and her associations with Chris as she could find. She cared little for anything else.

Despite herself, with Charlie's graphic description she felt the first flickering of interest—the huge population of itinerant loggers, the tiny settled community of locals, dependent on the loggers for their survival and yet still resentful of their intrusive presence, the struggling families of the loggers, moving from place to place as the employment of their menfolk demanded. Charlie drew them with humorous anecdotes of his experiences over the years, and Alex soaked it in, knowing that such information could be invaluable in the future. Of Dr McIntyre, after his initial comments, he said little, obviously judging that it was up to Alex to make up her own mind.

The brief touchdowns for the picking up and setting down of passengers passed almost unnoticed until finally the stewardess came from her seat to warn them that they had arrived. In panic Alex broke her conversation with Charlie to gaze out of the window. The cleared airstrip cut a swathe through seemingly impenetrable bush. In the distance, smoke curled lazily upward through the mist from the tiny dots that must represent the cabins of the logging town. Suddenly Alex felt a surge of longing for her mother. Her mother's plaintive cry of, 'I don't see why you need to go so far from us,' rang in her ears and her good reasoned arguments disintegrated. Charlie's hand went firmly over hers.

'You're going to be fine. I'll not be seeing you back in Hobart in tears, I know.' He fingered her hand thoughtfully. With Charlie it seemed neither familiar nor irritating. On her third finger, Chris's ring still lay. He looked at her questioningly. 'Married, then?'

Alex looked down at the small circlet of gold, a memory of a lifetime ago. She fingered it and then gazed downward at the approaching runway. With a tug she pulled it off and slipped it into the pocket of her leather jacket.

'No,' she said firmly. 'Not any more.'

He grinned. 'Atta girl!' The plane touched down with a sudden bump. 'Go get 'em!'

CHAPTER TWO

THE door of the plane swung open as the stairs were pushed into place outside, and Alex flinched as the cold hit her full in the face. She would have to start this job in midwinter, she thought bitterly. The hostess bade them goodbye and swung the door heavily shut behind them, obviously grateful that it was they and not she who had to face the perils of Pirrengurra.

Charlie and Alex were left standing on the tarmac, waiting as their luggage was unloaded. Alex gazed thoughtfully around.

The airstrip was cut into a valley. The mist coated the whole scene, not too thickly to prevent her discerning the mountains looming up on all sides of them. The place looked cold, eerie and utterly desolate. Even the terminal building looked forlorn and uninviting in the stillness. Alex felt a desire to run. Behind them the aircraft lumbered off down the runway. The piercing noise reached crescendo, it accelerated and became airborne once again. Her last link was broken. After the ear-shattering noise of the plane, the quiet was palpable.

'I ordered the cab,' said Charlie. 'It should be here soon.'

'I was rather expecting to be met myself.' Alex perched herself on her upright suitcase, feeling very grateful for his comforting presence.

The stillness was broken by the sound of a Land Rover being driven at a spanking pace along the road into the strip. It turned towards them and came to a halt a few feet from where they were standing. The door swung open and a tall,

11

muffled figure jumped out.

'G'day, Charlie.' Alex had an impression of a deeply tanned face, a shock of fair hair and blue eyes crinkled into a grin. 'Whoops—sorry, mate, it's Roger Anson this time, isn't it? I know you ordered the taxi, but Pete's crook. The bank knew I was coming out, so they asked me to pick you up.'

Charlie gazed at him. 'How the hell? I booked under the name of one of the logging company directors this time, but they still picked it up. So much for my surprise inspection!' he ended, in disgust. He laughed and the big blond man joined in. 'Alex,' he turned to her, 'don't just stand there—touch your forelock or something. Alex Donell, this is Andrew McIntyre, your new boss.'

For the first time the big man's gaze centred on Alex. Briefly it left her and swept the now deserted tarmac, then came back to meet her eyes. His laughter died on his lips and he exclaimed incredulously, 'They haven't sent me another woman?'

Alex, her hand already stretched out in greeting, was left holding it in mid-air. A heavy silence fell, broken only by the soft chatter of the magpies in the trees behind the terminal. Andrew McIntyre gazed at Alex as if he could not believe his eyes, and finally exploded, his concentrated anger washing over Alex like icy water.

'I told them after the last one, no more. Alex!' He spat the name derisively. 'They've pulled the wool nicely over my eyes. Women are useless out here, useless!' He turned to Charlie. 'They come out here after some broken romance thinking what a great spot to pick up a husband, sit and simper at the surgery and run to me the first time a logger uses a four-letter word in front of them.' His eyes swept over Alex and fell on her left hand. Reaching up, he held it up for the three of them to see. Clearly etched against the tan was the white mark of Chris's ring, so recently removed.

'See what I mean? She'll either make up with the boyfriend and leave next week or sit and weep until some other poor devil falls for her!'

'Hey, Andrew!' Charlie's voice rose in protest. 'This one's not like the other.'

'They're all the same.' Andrew McIntyre raised his hand to his head in a gesture of exhaustion. 'All I need is someone who can work.'

Alex let her hand fall slowly to her side. The shock of her greeting hit like a physical slap as she fought futilely to keep a hold on her temper. Charlie's hand reached out to take her arm, but she shook it off. Her eyes didn't leave Andrew McIntyre's face. He reached down to pick up her suitcase, shoving it roughly in the back of the Land Rover.

'Just a moment!' Her voice cut like a whip. 'You can apologise before I so much as get into a vehicle with you. Of all the bigoted, boorish men I've ever met, you would appear to take the prize!'

'Get in.' Andrew McIntyre's face was set. He moved to the front of the vehicle and held open the door.

'No! We might as well start as we mean to go on. I came out to work, and work I intend to. My relationships have absolutely nothing to do with you and are none of your business. The job advertised was for a doctor, not for a man, or for a woman—or even,' her eyes met his, 'for a spoilt little boy without manners enough to greet a colleague with courtesy. I get an apology now or I go into the terminal and I order a charter flight back to Hobart at the company's expense, and I tell them that you refused to work with me, Dr

McIntyre.'

Charlie goggled. The silence intensified as the two glared at each other. Alex was aware that she was shaking, but her gaze didn't waver.

'It's your decision, Dr McIntyre.'

Andrew McIntyre's eyes closed in a gesture of defeat. Once again, through her anger, Alex sensed exhaustion, the signs of a man close to breaking-point. The capitulation, when it came, left her feeling strangely empty.

'OK, OK—I'm sorry.' With an effort he seemed to pull himself together. Belatedly he held out his hand. 'Welcome to Pirrengurra, Dr Donell. Prove me wrong. Please.'

Alex looked down at the extended hand. Anger and shock warred within her, but suddenly her overwhelming feeling was sadness. Her first impression of this man had been a sensation of expectation and of pleasure. His reaction to her had shattered the feeling, leaving her curiously bereft. She shook his hand, said nothing and climbed into the Land Rover.

The drive into Pirrengurra was mercifully brief, with Charlie keeping up a strained effort at small talk from the back seat. The roads were tortuous hairpin bends with steep rock faces on one side and sharp drops on the other. It took two days' drive to get from Pirrengurra to the east coast, and Alex was beginning to realise why. One day, though, if Andrew McIntyre was driving, she thought. He seemed to be taking his anger out on the Land Rover, and she was forced to hold on to her seat with both hands as he rounded the sharper bends.

'We should have kept some of those nice handy little paper bags from the plane,' she joked with Charlie. Charlie grinned and held his stomach expressively. Andrew McIntyre glanced sideways at her, then straight ahead again. He didn't slow down. Wow, Dr McIntyre, you're going to be a fun person to work with, I don't think! she thought.

They dropped Charlie on the footpath outside the bank.

'It's a wonder the manager hasn't got a guard of honour lined up outside,' he said. 'Here goes, then. Surprise, surprise!' He leaned into Alex's window before the Land Rover pulled away. 'I'm in town for a few days. Find me at the bank during the day or the pub at night if you need me.' He reached in and gripped her hand. 'Good luck.'

He stepped back as the Land Rover roared off.

'Made a conquest already, then?'

Alex flushed and said nothing. The comment hung in the air between them. She knew she was close to tears, but was determined not to give in to them. Andrew McIntyre glanced across at her, then swore.

'I'm sorry, I didn't mean that. Charlie's a thoroughly nice guy.'

'I know that,' she said. 'Why the gibe?'

He ran his hand through his hair. 'I said I'm sorry. Look, I'm being a bloody oaf, but the truth is that I haven't slept for three nights, I've got a woman in labour now who looks like she'll deliver at three in the morning and an afternoon's schedule that'd make a city doctor pass out with horror. I've been counting on getting some help, and now——' He broke off.

'And now you've got a woman instead of a man. I've said it before, Dr McIntyre . . .'

'Andrew.'

'OK—Andrew, then. I came here to work. Just start treating me as a doctor and not as something in a skirt.' Alex gazed down at her wide baggy trousers and grinned. Looking up she caught the beginnings of a smile cross his face.

The Land Rover was pulling over, and Alex looked out to see a long white building set back on well-kept lawns. They pulled into a reserved parking space, next to a vehicle similar but decidedly older than the one they were in. Andrew reached into his pocket and threw Alex a set of keys.

'Your wheels,' he said. The job had been advertised as 'car provided' and he sat waiting for her reaction. He obviously expected her to be disappointed, but in fact Alex was delighted. She had enjoyed the four-wheel-drive vehicles when she lived up north and the battered little jalopy already had the air of being an old friend.

'That's terrific!' she smiled.

Andrew stared at her, doubting the sincerity of her reaction, then shrugged and opened his door. They retrieved Alex's luggage and walked across the path to the hospital entrance.

A sister, starchly white with a warm welcoming smile, came across to greet them.

Andrew was brusque.

'Janet, this Dr Donell. Can I leave her with you?' He turned to Alex. 'I have to go. Sister Davis will show you where your accommodation is.' He put the cases down and disappeared down the corridor.

Alex gazed after him, trying to sort out the mixture of her emotions. How was she ever going to establish a working relationship with him?

She realised the other girl was eyeing her with a mixture of curiosity and delight.

'Hi. I'm Janet Davis.' A hand was thrust welcomingly at her. 'You're supposed to be a man.'

'So I've been told.' Alex returned the grip. 'Please call me

Alex. I hope you're not appalled as well?'

Janet grinned, a big, infectious grin that lit her whole face.

'Not me! There are some around here who are going to be not too pleased, though.'

'Meaning Dr McIntyre?'

'And another I could mention,' Janet added mysteriously. 'But I won't. There'll be time enough for you to find that out! Come on and I'll show you your quarters.'

She seized a suitcase and led the way. Alex picked up the other case and followed her.

Her apartment was a neat little flat attached to the rear of the hospital. A door led off from the hospital sunroom, leading into two pleasant rooms, a bedroom and a kitchen/living area with french windows opening on to the lawns beyond. A tiny bathroom completed the suite, and Alex gazed around in pleasure. It was bright, comfortably furnished and newly painted. After her digs in the city it seemed like a mansion. Janet was watching her anxiously.

'Is it OK? You can always move out and find a place in town if you like, but it's easier for us if you live here.'

'It's perfect,' Alex assured her.

'Great! Look, I have to go. There's everything you need, I think, and if there's not just give a yell to the hospital kitchen. Mrs Mac's a love. For the price of a morsel of gossip she'll supply you with all you could possibly want in the way of food. She makes the best lamingtons this side of the Tasman and treats us all as if we're pathetically undernourished.' Janet flicked her apron straight, gave Alex another of her infectious grins and departed.

Alex walked into the bedroom. The bed looked soft and inviting. The strain of the long journey from Brisbane and her reception when she had finally arrived had taken their toll.

Just a few moments' rest before I start unpacking, she told herself. She settled on to the pretty blue counterpane and fell fast asleep.

When she woke the last of the light had faded. Momentarily confused, she pushed herself upright and sat trying to get her bearings. A loud banging echoed through the flat. Alex pushed her hand wearily through her hair and went to the door.

Outside stood the hospital matron. One glance was enough to establish her position. Although her uniform was almost identical to Janet's, the sister she had just met, there was no possibility of mistaking the different ranks of the two girls. This lady exuded authority. She was short, much shorter than Alex, trim and immaculate. Nothing was out of place, from the tips of her perfectly manicured nails to the intricate arrangement of her blonde hair, piled in perfectly behaved curls on top of her head. Alex was aware of the crumpled appearance she must present, still in her leather jacket and crushed trousers with her hair tousled and make-up no longer existent. The other girl's face was politely expressionless.

'Dr Donell?'

'Yes.' Who else could I be? thought Alex nastily. She pulled herself together. 'Call me Alex, please. I must have fallen asleep.'

'Yes.' An expression of total uninterest. 'I'm Matron Nash. We have a small problem we wondered if you could help us with?' She ended on a note of interrogation and doubt.

Alex pulled herself wide awake.

'Of course. What's the problem?'

'We've a logger who's just come in with a cut on his leg. It needs stitches. Andrew's out at Kinley with afternoon surgery and I don't really like to leave this much longer.'

'Messing up your clean floor, is he, Matron?' Alex asked with a smile. As soon as she said it she realised it was a mistake. The other woman stared at her as if she were some lowly form of animal species usually cleaned up with disinfectant. Whoops! thought Alex. I think I need to go carefully here.

'Of course I'll come,' she said hurriedly.

'It shouldn't take too long, then you can get back to your nap.'

Alex flushed.

'Give me a minute,' she said. 'I need a wash before I do anything.'

'There are white coats supplied. There'll be a couple hanging in your wardrobe.' Matron Nash looked pointedly at Alex's leather jacket.

'Fine.' Two minutes later Alex joined her in the corridor.

Without a word, the other woman turned and made her way along the polished floors. Alex dug her hands into her coat pockets and hurried to keep up.

'I didn't catch your name?' she queried as they turned in the direction of the theatre.

'Matron Nash.' She swung the door open and motioned for Alex to go in. 'This is our small theatre, Alex.'

Alex took a deep breath. 'Dr Donell, please, Matron.' She swept past.

The theatre was small, set up especially for dealing with minor surgery. One glance around showed that it had been designed with care and was superbly equipped. Alex started to relax.

On the couch lay a huge man, grimy and weatherbeaten. He looked decidedly sorry for himself. Alex gave him a quick smile and introduced herself before turning her attention to the wound. It was on the side of his calf, jagged and ugly but not too deep.

'How did you manage this?' she asked with interest.

'Heaving timber. You get 'em all the time,' he explained. 'You just try to move a bit of the light rubbish yourself and you get scratched to blazes. The boss thought I ought to get this one checked out.'

Alex raised her head and smiled into his anxious face.

'It's actually not quite as bad as it looks,' she said reassuringly. 'It's ragged, but not too deep. I think we can get quite a satisfactory result just by taping the wound together.' The man's countenance lightened. Alex turned to Matron. 'Could you bring me some steri strips, please?'

She turned back to the wound, but realised the girl hadn't moved.

'You have steri strips, Matron?'

'Yes.'

Alex turned to face her. 'Is there a problem?'

'Dr McIntyre would like a cut of this size stitched, please, Doctor.'

Alex searched the other girl's face. It remained impassive. She turned again to the patient, who was eyeing the two of them in doubt.

'If stitches are the best way to go then stitches it ought to be, Doc.' He gave a half-hearted grin. 'I don't mind a bit of pain. What's a needle or two between friends?'

'I'm sure you're a real hero,' Alex smiled at him, 'but stitches really aren't necessary. The skin will be held very firmly in place by the steri strips. With a wound like this you often get a better result than if you use stitches.' Without looking backward, she repeated her request.

'Get me the steri strips, please, Matron.'

She was aware of an angry silence, then footsteps receding and returning. The strips were put into her hand and the rest of the procedure passed without incident. As the big man got up to leave he grasped her hand.

'Thanks, Doc. A real neat job, I reckon.' He paused and glanced at Matron. 'Much better'n stitches, I reckon.' He swung himself down from the couch and departed.

Alex was left facing the other girl. Much of her anger had evaporated in the time it took to dress the wound, but she was still aware of the woman's blatant hostility. Taking the bull by the horns, she started.

'Matron, when has it become nursing practice to question the doctor's decisions in front of the patient?'

Matron swept to the door and opened it. 'I'll clean up here, Doctor. Sister will show you where the kitchens are if you'd like a meal.'

'You haven't answered my question.'

Matron's face set. 'You'll find here, Dr Donell, that there is only one set of rules, the rules imposed by Dr McIntyre. It will be better for you if you accept them early on in your *training*.' She put a heavy emphasis on the word 'training'.

Alex paused for a moment before replying. When she did she spoke softly, trying to hold anger in check.

'Matron, I am not "in training". I am a fully fledged doctor with all the appropriate qualifications to prove it. Dr McIntyre's patients are his business and you will of course follow orders from him. My patients will be treated by the methods deemed suitable by me. Dr McIntyre will not interfere.'

'Will not interfere with what?'

With a shock Alex realised the door was still open and their voices were sounding down the corridor. Andrew McIntyre strode into the room. He glanced from one set face to the other and sighed.

'Well, I see you two have got to know each other. Is there a problem?'

Alex flushed.

Matron smiled and replied with composure, 'Not at all, Andrew. Just letting Alex know what you'll expect of her. Excuse me.' She smiled sweetly and left the room.

Andrew closed his eyes in a gesture of irritation. 'Please don't get the nursing staff offside! I've got a first-rate team of nurses here, and the last thing I need is trouble.'

Alex gasped with the injustice of his remark, but before she could respond Janet's welcome face appeared around the door. She glanced curiously from one to the other.

'Matron said you'd be ready for some tea, Alex. Coming?'

Alex gave her colleague an angry glance and left the room.

Janet showed her through to the kitchens and introduced her to Mrs Mac, a motherly soul with a face alive with friendly interest. She bustled about them, plying them with more food than they could possibly need, clucked over Alex's slim figure and finally disappeared. The homely sound of saucepans clattering and splashing wafted through the open door.

Janet's company was soothing. She accepted Alex's lack of interest in talking and rambled happily about the hospital and its personalities. Her gossip was informative but not malicious. She obviously loved her job, and her respect for Andrew showed through in every word she spoke of him.

'He'll probably take you up to Brawton tomorrow afternoon. I think the plan is that you take over Brawton completely.'

'Brawton?' queried Alex.

'One of the logging camps,' Janet enlightened her. 'There are two big ones, Kinley and Brawton. Kinley's about thirty minutes north of the town and Brawton's about twenty minutes south-west. We've found it pays to have clinics there rather than have them all come into the town with the doctor still having to go out for the odd one who's too sick to come in.' She paused. 'It's a rotten trip if you're already feeling unwell.'

Alex nodded agreement.

'You'll be taking over Brawton,' Janet continued. 'At least, that was the plan until we realised you were female.'

'And now?'

'I dunno!' Janet held up her hands helplessly. 'I just work here, lady.'

Alex laughed and went to bed.

At two in the morning the phone rang beside her bed. She was still wide awake, lying staring into the darkness.

'Alex? Andrew here. Your application said you had obstetric and anaesthetic experience. Was that another lie?'

Alex was speechless.

'Alex?'

'I did not lie on my application!' Her voice came out a squeak. 'Did you ring me up at two in the morning to question me——?'

She was cut off. 'Which do you prefer, anaesthetics or surgery?'

She was sitting up now.

'What's going on?' she demanded.

'This delivery's going wrong. The mother needs a Caesar. I can fly her to Hobart, but the baby'll be dead before she gets there.'

'What are we waiting for?' Alex was already out of bed.

'Which?' Andrew McIntyre asked.

'I'll cut.'

By the time she reached the theatre the patient was ready. As she scrubbed Alex tensed up. Was she stupid to elect to cut? Her mental review of the procedure started in her head without her willing it to.

Thirty minutes later a fine little boy was letting his displeasure at his rough treatment be known. For the first time since she stepped on to the plane Alex felt herself relax. The tension drained out of her as she looked at the tiny baby's perfect features. The mother, still sedated but awake, smiled sleepily. Her husband, another huge logger, was grinning with delight. Suddenly Alex had had enough. Tears welled up and overflowed. As the night sister looked on in amazement, Alex choked on a sob and ran from the room. Andrew was left gazing after her, a look of total disbelief on his face.

CHAPTER THREE

ALEX slept late and woke to the knowledge that someone was in the room. The curtains were being flung aside and the smell of fresh brewed coffee wafted through the air. Alex opened one eye and cautiously investigated. Janet. She sat up and followed the message her nose was giving her. Bacon and eggs, hot, buttery toast and a pot of coffee. Heaven!

'I can't afford this hotel,' she complained.

Janet giggled.

'Compliments of Dr McIntyre. You should have seen Matron's face when he said we were to bring it in to you!' She plonked the tray on the bed and perched on the end. 'The Lawson baby is doing beautifully, thanks to you, but even Dr McIntyre seems to think it was a bit hard to have to wake you up on your first night here.'

'It was my first unsupervised Caesar,' Alex admitted, 'although I'd be grateful if you didn't let Matron know that. She already thinks I'm some sort of nasty student being.'

Immediately she said it she regretted it, but Janet was eyeing her with respect as well as sympathy.

'She does it to us all. I'm just as qualified as Margaret Nash—I'm a triple certificate sister,' Janet's voice had an edge of pride to it, 'yet she treats me like a probationer at times. I shouldn't be here. I could have my own hospital if I was prepared to leave, but my mum and dad are still in the valley, and to tell you the truth there's nowhere I'd rather be.'

25

'Some people have weird tastes.' Alex smiled to take any offence from her words, and Janet grinned back.

'Each to their own. Where are you from?'

'Brisbane.' Alex's voice tightened, waiting for follow up questions, but Janet was not about to interrogate her.

'I don't know how you stand the heat! Give me nice cold Tasmania any day, where a girl can appreciate her hot-water bottle.' She rose and walked to the door. 'Dr McIntyre had to leave early and go up-country with the ambulance— someone's come off his horse. He asked if you could do a brief ward round; we've only got twelve in, so it shouldn't take long, and could you run the morning clinic at ten? He said he'd give you a proper tour when he got back. Could you be ready to start in half an hour?'

'I haven't got any excuse now, have I?' Alex swallowed the last morsel of toast and reached for the coffee-pot. 'Away with you, slave-driver, and let the slave get on with it!'

Janet was already out of the door.

As the door shut Alex was out of bed and heading for the shower, mentally reviewing her wardrobe. Casual and efficient, she thought, though after her shower as she rummaged through her half-unpacked bags she found she had little choice. In the end it came down to the outfit that least needed a press, a tight-fitting deep green skirt with a soft green blouse buttoning high at her throat, pale green court shoes and her white medical coat over the top. She eyed herself critically in the mirror. Normally she didn't take pains over her appearance, but today it seemed important. She pinned her hair severely back and frowned at the unruly wisps which refused to be tamed. They curled in tiny tendrils around her face, giving the lie to her bid for a stern, efficient appearance. Never mind, time was up. The day had begun.

Matron was waiting for her in the nurses' station. They

greeted each other politely.

'Andrew asked me to show you around the wards. Would you follow me, Doctor?'

Alex fell in meekly behind.

The hospital was beautifully run. The place gleamed. Alex was forced to admit that if Margaret Nash was responsible for the day-to-day running of the hospital she was doing an extraordinary job. Her standards were such as few city hospitals could match.

In every ward Margaret introduced Alex to the patients. Alex tried to greet each of them, but was whisked away by her companion. She was left with the impression that Margaret was held in respect by the patients, but Charlie's comments about 'a cold piece of work' came to mind. In the children's ward a small boy had dropped his blocks from the bed, and Margaret made a small noise of irritation and went forward to pick them up, not interrupting her flow of talk to Alex. Alex had a brief impression of a sad little waif of a child before Margaret led her away.

Mrs Lawson was delighted to see Alex. Comfortably in bed, with her son in his crib beside her, she beamed with pleasure at her two visitors.

'We're so grateful to you, Doctor, my husband and me. This is our first and we've been trying for ages. If anything had happened to him,' she gazed down into the crib, 'eh, it doesn't bear thinking of.' She looked up at Alex. 'And you so tired. All the way from Brisbane, Dr McIntyre tell us, and then to be called out in the middle of the night. I don't wonder it got a bit much for you!'

Behind her Margaret made a small noise of impatience, and Alex wondered what version she had been given of the night's events. She smiled happily down at the pair lying close together.

'What will you call him?' she asked.

'Peter, we think. And Thomas for his dad.'

Alex put a hand down and snuggled it against a tiny cheek. 'Welcome to the world, Peter Thomas. Now, let's have a look at your mum's tummy.'

'Dr McIntyre will check Mrs Lawson when he returns.' Margaret's voice cut authoritatively over them.

'I'm sure he will,' Alex agreed, willing herself to keep calm, 'but meanwhile I'm sure Mrs Lawson won't mind me checking my handiwork.' She smiled gently down at the lady in question, who smiled back.

'Go right ahead, Doctor. If it's all the same to you I wouldn't mind if you did all the looking. It's not that I don't like Dr McIntyre, I think he's lovely, it's just that—well . . .'

'He's a man and I'm not.' Alex laughed. 'It really shouldn't worry you, but we do understand, don't we, Matron?' She turned to Margaret, who was forced to give a wintry little smile. 'I'll talk to Dr McIntyre about it later and see what he says. I'm a bit new here to go about pinching patients!'

The rest of the tour passed uneventfully. Alex tried determinedly to pass pleasantries with Margaret, but the woman seemed totally opposed to any sort of idle chatter. What have I done to upset her so much? Alex thought. This is going to be impossible. She was relieved at ten o'clock to be handed over to Janet.

'Sister Davis will assist you during morning surgery.' Margaret disappeared into her office, leaving Alex with a deep sense of unease. For some reason she had an enemy. She could not understand the hostility she was meeting.

Janet was waiting with a clipboard under her arm. She seemed almost apprehensive to see Alex and her normal smile had slipped.

'Is something wrong?' Alex queried.

'It's the morning surgery,' Janet explained.

'There's a problem?'

Janet bit her lip. 'Well, not exactly a problem. I mean—well, yes, there is, actually. Normally this surgery has only a few patients. We'd consider ten a fair morning.'

'And this morning?'

Janet's voice dropped to a whisper. 'Thirty-five. And Alex, apart from Mrs Jefferson and her three kids, they're all loggers!'

They looked at each other.

'Perhaps we have an epidemic on our hands.' Alex gave Janet a reassuring grin. 'Have they all got spots?'

'I'm not a doctor,' Janet's voice approached normal again, 'but they all look disgustingly healthy to me.'

'Let's go and find out.' The two girls braced themselves and stepped through into the outpatients' waiting-room.

The room was packed. In one corner of the room, wedged against the wall, was a tiny, gaunt little woman with a baby in her arms and two small children clinging as close to her skirt as they could. The rest of the room was taken up with men; big, rugged men in tough outdoor gear. As Alex entered their heads swung round towards her. A long, low whistle of appreciation sounded from somewhere near the back of the room. Alex blushed before their concerted gaze and fled into the surgery.

'It doesn't take long for the word to get around! Would you like me to tell them to clear out?' Janet was indignant.

'No.' Alex sat at the desk, toying with her pen. 'Let me think about it. I'd better see Mrs Jefferson first, though. She looks uncomfortable, to say the least.'

By the time Alex had coped with the various coughs, sneezes and sniffles of the three small Jeffersons she had decided that the loggers should be seen. They had made individual appointments, so it was almost an admission of defeat to dismiss them all . Besides, somewhere among them perhaps there was a genuine problem. Janet called the first one in, a strapping young blond man built like a tank. He sat down in the chair opposite her, arms folded, enjoying himself immensely.

'Can I help you in some way?' asked Alex.

'Gee, Doc, I hope so.' He gave a pathetic sigh and then looked up to see how she reacted. 'I've got this terrible headache, right here it is.' He clutched his forehead expressively.

'Do you get these headaches often?'

'Never before, Doc, cross my heart. Something terrible, it is!'

Alex walked around the desk. She bent down and checked his eyes. Through the ophthalmoscope, the eyes gazed at her hopefully.

'Is it something serious, Doc? Perhaps I need a bit of bed rest with you looking after me.' He returned her gaze innocently.

Alex put two fingers lightly on his forehead. 'This pain, is it here?'

His hand reached out to cover hers. 'Just up a bit, Doc. You can feel the pulse pounding up there.'

Alex carefully disengaged his hand. 'Well, you know, I think we can manage without the bed rest.' She turned to Janet. 'Sister, could you bring me the large brain needle, please?'

Janet looked up. 'The brain needle?'

Alex looked directly at her. 'Yes, please, Sister.'

Janet looked again at Alex, went to say something and then thought better of it. 'There's one in theatre, Doctor. I won't be a moment.'

'Leave the door open,' Alex added. 'It's stuffy in here.'

Janet left. Through the open door thirty pairs of eyes watched with interest. Alex turned to the sink. In the large cupboard below she found what she was looking for. By the time Janet returned a beaker of brilliant crimson solution was mixed and waiting on the bench. Alex had her head down, writing on her prescription pad. Without raising her head, she said, 'Prepare it, please, Sister.' She waved a hand at the solution and went back to her writing.

Two minutes later Janet was finished. Alex stood up and took the needle from her. It was huge. The needle itself measured perhaps five inches long. Alex held it up to the lamp. The fluid in the syringe showed red against the light. With a sigh she put it down again.

'Not this one, Sister. I said the large brain needle.'

A tiny noise, not unlike a whimper, came from the chair.

'I'm sorry,' Alex leaned forward, 'I missed that.'

The young giant rose unsteadily to his feet and looked from one to the other.

'Doc, if it's all the same to you,' he backed towards the door while talking, 'I think I'll just go back to camp and take an aspirin.'

He went.

Alex followed him thoughtfully to the door and leaned against the door-jamb, fingering the syringe idly between her fingers.

'Next?'

They looked at her and they looked at the syringe. There

was silence, followed by embarrassed laughter and a few sheepish grins. Slowly the room cleared.

There were two who remained, and their complaints were genuine. The first came in and cast a nervous glance at the syringe, lying on the bench. Janet had her back turned. She was doubled up with laughter. Temporarily useless as a nurse or anything else, Alex thought, trying hard to retain control over her own features.

'Can I help you?' she asked.

Again, a nervous glance. 'Well, Doc, I haven't got a headache.'

It was too much. The girls subsided into paroxysms of laughter. The patient laughed too, with just a hint of relief in his laughter.

Alex attended to his infected finger and his friend's stitches which needed removing and morning surgery was finished. Janet was still choking as they bade farewell to the last patient and Andrew walked in.

'Can I share the joke?' he queried.

Janet picked up the syringe and waved it joyfully over her head. 'Alex has just cured thirty patients with the use of one small brain needle. Heavens, Dr McIntyre, imagine what she could do with a big one?' She carried it out, still laughing.

Andrew leaned against the wall and regarded Alex with amusement. 'I heard, actually. I met some of the loggers coming out. I hope these aren't city ideas on how to treat a headache?'

He was smiling as he said it, but Alex still flushed. This man unsettled her. He went on, 'Thank you for last night, and I do have to apologise. I would have been well served if you'd got on a charter flight back to Hobart.'

Alex cast a nervous glance at him. He was still smiling. A

warm glow settled inside her and spread.

'Would you care to do another ward round with me?' he asked. 'I know Margaret has taken you around, but I would like to explain a few things to you myself.'

This round was different. For the first time the man beside her seemed relaxed and at ease, and what a difference it made! Alex found herself casting little sidelong glances at him, waiting for the frown to come down over his eyes.

She noticed the difference in the ward as they entered. When she and Margaret had walked in, early this morning, a silence had descended on each room. With Andrew the reverse was the case as each patient welcomed him with pleasure. Even the little boy in the children's ward, his face blank and lost, raised his eyes and followed Andrew's movements. Andrew sat on his bed and started to fiddle with the blocks, lying abandoned on the bedside table where Matron had placed them hours previously. While he talked, the blocks started to form a shape.

'You're getting on really well, Rob. Another couple of weeks and your mum and dad will be able to come and take you home.'

Silence. The small face pushed itself back into the pillows and watched.

'It might be a little while before you can kick the footy around, though. That's going to be hard.' Alex's voice was sympathetic. 'Still, I reckon by your seventh birthday—let's see, that's only two months off—you should be back to kicking. Want me to tell your mum to organise a new ball?'

The eyes, still distrustful, moved imperceptibly in agreement.

'I haven't played since I came to Pirrengurra,' Andrew went on regretfully. 'Too busy. And this lady, she comes from

Brisbane, and she's never seen Australian Rules there.'

Two faces turned to her, full of the enormity of all Alex had missed out on. 'What team does your dad play for, Rob?' Andrew went on.

A whisper. 'Kinley Reserves.'

'Well, mate, why don't we make a date? The first Saturday afternoon you're out of this place why don't you and I take Dr Donell to the football? We'll give the lady a treat, eh?'

The eyes looked from one face to the other. This time the smile reached Rob's eyes and stayed there. 'OK.'

'Right, it's a date.' Andrew swung his long legs down from the bed. He looked down at his hands, as if remembering what he had been doing. The blocks were shaped into a multi-coloured rocket. 'Sorry, mate, I've been fiddling with your blocks.'

'That's OK.' Rob's voice was gracious. He reached out a hand and took the rocket. It disappeared under the bedclothes, obviously to be inspected more closely once these intrusive adults had departed.

Alex fought to suppress a smile, and they left together.

A brief call on Mrs Lawson, where Andrew laughed at Alex's professional scruples in pinching patients, and the hospital tour was finished. They walked down the corridor together.

'Would you like to go down into the town for lunch?' asked Andrew. 'There's a fantastic choice of eating places — the pub, the pub or, if you want to be really extravagant, there's the pub.'

'Lovely,' Alex agreed with a feeling of lightness in her heart. Perhaps this job was going to work out after all.

'And which of the three will it be?'

'The third, of course.' She didn't hesitate. 'I only go for

the best.'

They were still laughing as Margaret came out of her office to meet them.

'Andrew, there you are!' Her smile was lovely, reaching out intimately to centre his attention on her.

'Margaret. We're off down town for lunch.' Andrew's return smile was just as warm, Alex noted, then she caught herself. What was she doing? 'Care to join us?'

'Oh, sweetheart, we can't!' A quick pitying glance at Alex. 'Those path. results have just come through from Hobart and I've got several queries on this month's figures which have to be looked at before tonight's board meeting. I've ordered lunch for us in my office.' Her tone excluded Alex nicely. 'Mrs Mac does lunch for the staff in the kitchen,' she added for Alex's benefit.

If she says 'Run along, dear' I'll hit her! Alex thought. Out loud, she replied calmly, 'I think I still might go down town. I've been here for twenty-four hours and I've only seen the airport and the hospital.'

Andrew gave her an apologetic smile.

'Sorry, Alex. Tomorrow, perhaps. The pub is right in the centre of the main street — you can't miss it. Just keep on going downhill.' He looked at his watch. 'Don't be too long, though. We've got clinic at Brawton at two.'

Alex stopped at her flat to collect a jacket and went out to investigate her vehicle. It hadn't improved in appearance overnight. A smart little Porsche, gleaming white, parked beside it in the space marked Matron, made it seem all the more dilapidated. Alex swung herself in. It greeted her with the smell of an old and tried vehicle. She settled herself back in the driver's seat. It fitted her like an old glove. She stuck her tongue out at the gleaming Porsche and turned the key. The stillness of the valley was shattered. Obviously the muffler wasn't all that it should be. Her car wasn't going to sneak up on anybody!

The pub was easy to find, the largest building in a town of perhaps a dozen shops. She roared into the car park, turning every head in sight. Lots of girls would be intimidated by this, she thought, but not me. Fighting to keep the mounting colour from her face, she pushed open the lounge door.

Silence fell. Every head turned in her direction. Alex stood with a growing sense of panic inside her. I can't cope, she thought. There's nothing wrong with a sandwich in my flat. Suddenly a voice called from near the bar.

'Alex!'

Alex swung towards the voice. Beaming his way towards her was Charlie Taylor. She had never been so grateful to see anyone in her life. In two minutes they were seated together at a table and the throb of conversation started up again.

The menu was great — steak and chips, pie with chips, chops with chips or sausages and chips.

'You should come here on Friday, though.' Charlie dropped his voice in awe.

'What happens on Friday?'

'Fish and chips!'

'Wow!'

She settled for the steak. When it came a slice of tender rump covered the dinner plate, almost three inches thick. A mountain of chips were heaped on top.

Charlie grinned, 'You should see what happens when you order a large one!'

While Alex plodded her way through Charlie held forth,

seemingly as pleased to see her as she was to see him.

'We've been hearing nothing else except "the new lady doctor" all morning. The town's agog,' he twinkled. 'It seems you've cured the entire population of headaches for years to come!'

Alex blushed. 'I shouldn't have done it. I was very sure he was putting it on.'

'Nothing surer,' Charlie agreed. 'You have to realise that the men outweigh the women in this community ten to one and almost all the female population are married or still in pigtails or nappies. A new young woman in town, whatever she does, brings comments, and to have one as accessible as you are is bound to cause——' He broke off.

'Trouble?'

'Well, let's just say I think a man would have less trouble being accepted.'

'I know that,' Alex had to agree. 'Perhaps I was stupid to come here. But now I am here,' she set her face resolutely, 'I mean to give it my best shot.'

'Good for you!' He raised his beer glass. 'Here's to your success.'

'Thanks, Charlie.'

She finished the last of her coffee and stood up to leave. As she did so the barman appeared.

'Doc McIntyre on the phone, miss.'

'Thank you.' Alex followed the man back to the pay phone on the end of the bar. She winced as the voice at the other end barked into the phone.

'Where the hell are you?'

'I've only just finished my lunch.' She glanced at her watch. She had been gone for three quarters of an hour.

The voice at the other end continued as if it hadn't heard

her.

'We should be leaving now.'

'OK, OK, hold on to your hat!' She put the phone down, gave Charlie a quick wave of farewell across the room and headed for the door. The noise of her Land Rover echoed up the street. Two minutes later she roared into the hospital car park.

Andrew was out at the front. He winced as Alex turned off the ignition. At least the noise was something that was not her fault, she decided as she extricated herself from the Land Rover. His frown deepened, however, and by the time she reached him he was back to his icy self.

'Do you think you're going to be any good to me up at Brawton dressed like a fashion plate?'

Alex looked down at her clothes, feeling stunned.

'The place is knee-deep in mud,' he said, emphasising each word as though speaking to a particularly stupid child. 'Those pretty shoes would disappear under the surface before we made it from the Land Rover to the first hut.' He glanced at his watch. 'You have two minutes. Get something sensible on.' His voice had risen in anger. He wheeled away and started loading gear into the back of his vehicle.

Alex fled.

When she returned, only slightly over the stipulated time, she was wearing her big trousers, a large red pullover and leather boots, with her old leather jacket slung over her shoulder. Andrew stared at her critically as she climbed into the car.

'You call that sensible?' he demanded.

'What on earth is wrong now? Should I be wearing dungarees?' She flushed in anger.

Andrew looked at her again, made as if to say something

and then stopped. An uneasy silence was maintained in the car for the twenty-minute drive.

The scenery made up for the silence. The roads were narrow, sliced into the side of the majestic peaks looming over them. The bush towered above the road. In the brief stretches where the ground didn't drop away on one side of the road the towering gums with their thick mat of ferns as undergrowth made it seem as if the Land Rover was travelling through a tunnel. Patches of mist periodically enveloped the car, giving a mystic sense of unreality to the terrain. In rare moments, the bush and the mist fell away, granting a brief glimpse of snow-capped peaks high in the distance. Alex was content to hold her peace and soak in the country. She was aware of Andrew's attention. Every now and then she felt his puzzled glance on her before it moved back to the road.

The car wasn't heated. Before long she had her jacket on and found its old folds comforting and warm. The jacket was too big for her, she knew, but it was one of the few things of Chris's that she had retained. This man beside her disturbed her. She drew the jacket closer, almost as a shield.

Brawton was a rough jumble of huts, set in a sea of mud. The Land Rover's wheels spun as they drew in beside the first hut.

'Goodness, how do they cope with all their vehicles in this mess?' exclaimed Alex.

'They throw gravel down periodically,' Andrew was already out of the Land Rover and squelching his way to the back for his gear, 'but it soon disappears. The one thing they aren't short of here is men to push. You've come at a bad time. It's not always as wet as this.' He tossed her a large black bag. 'We had this made up for you — everything you'll be likely to need. After today you'll be on your own up here, but today I thought we'd split the patients. If you need anything, just yell.'

They made their way into the main hut where a section of the mess hall had been partitioned off for their use. The camp boss was there to greet them and formally welcomed Alex.

'We don't seem to have any headaches for you to see, though, Doc,' he informed her with a twinkle, and she blushed. That incident was going to take some living down!

They settled down to see a steady stream of men, and Alex was relieved that the illnesses were genuine and they were taking her seriously. After an hour or so she began to relax. Apart from the surroundings she could just as easily be in Outpatients back in Brisbane.

She had just finished examining the chest of an elderly man with a persistent cough when the door burst open and a tousle-haired youth appeared. He appealed directly to Andrew.

'Doc, can you come? It's Murdoch.'

Andrew looked up briefly from the wound he was dressing.

'What's the problem?' His attention went back to the gauze he was applying.

'He's got an asthma attack. He's been crook for a couple of days, but he reckoned it was just a cold. This afternoon he's worse. He's lying there gasping and he looks awful.'

'Does he want our help?' Andrew's voice was hard, and Alex looked at him in surprise.

The boy spread his hands helplessly.

'You know what he's like, Doc. He hates doctors.'

'Last time I offered to help,' Andrew said drily, 'I was told exactly where to go and what would happen if I didn't. You tell Murdoch to let us know if he wants us.'

'He's really bad, Doc.'

Alex stood up. She had just finished seeing a patient.

'I'll go,' she said.

Andrew looked up at her and shook his head.

'Alex, he's a severe asthmatic who won't admit he gets asthma. He's a huge man and he's prone to attacking anyone who interferes with him. Doctors, according to Murdoch, do just that.' He rose. 'Can you finish here? If he's as bad as his friend here thinks then I'd better see him.'

'No.' Alex shut her bag with a snap and motioned the boy towards the door. 'You're busy. I'm finished for the moment.'

His gaze held her speculatively, a sardonic grin lurking behind his eyes.

'Proving yourself, Dr Donell?'

Alex flushed and stalked out, slamming the door behind her.

They found Murdoch in one of the far huts. He lay like a beached whale, his huge form almost hiding the bed. His breath came in whistling gasps as he fought for each lungful of air. As Alex approached he raised his head weakly.

'Who the hell are you?'

'I'm a doctor.'

'I don't need a bloody doctor.'

Alex put her bag down on the cabinet beside the bed and opened it. She reached in for her stethoscope and adjusted it in her ears.

'I think perhaps you do.' Her tone was carefully calculated, a mixture of kindness and confidence.

With an effort Murdoch raised himself on one elbow. With his other arm he reached out and shoved her bag as hard as he could. It hit the floor, the contents scattering and spilling over the rough wooden floorboards.

Alex looked at the mess on the floor and then back to the bed. It had taken all the strength the man had. His face was a sickly blue and he was fighting to get the next breath. Behind her, Alex heard the door open as more men came into the hut. They stayed where they were, against the wall at the doorway, watching.

She reached down, her eyes still on the bed, and gathered her equipment. She found what she was looking for. Out of range of Murdoch, she prepared an injection and held it up for him to see.

'Two cowards in one day,' she said softly.

Murdoch's eyes flew to her face. His face was distorted with the effort of breathing.

'What do you mean?' he gasped.

'I had a lad in this morning who was afraid of a little needle.' She heard a choking behind her and allowed herself to grin. 'Now I've got another one.'

'I'm not scared of a bloody needle!'

'No?' Alex put it back in her bag. 'Within fifteen minutes of an injection your breathing would be easier. Mind you, to get proper relief you'd have to get the boys to drive you into hospital and spend a day or so on a drip — but I guess you're afraid of that too.' She closed her bag and started to turn away.

'Doc?' The man's voice was a mixture of fear and resignation.

'Yes?'

'Give me the shot.'

Alex made no move.

'You'll go to hospital?'

He gestured impatiently.

'Yes, I'll go to bloody hospital. Give me the shot.'

Alex grinned and opened her bag. She listened briefly to his chest, then administered the injection. Murdoch relaxed back against the pillows, and she smiled down at him.

'Didn't hurt a bit, did it?'

He gave a sheepish smile, still concentrating on the struggle to take one breath after another.

She turned to the men at the door.

'Can one of you——?' She stopped. Andrew was lounging against the wall, his hands in his pockets and an expression of amusement on his face. She bit her lip.

'Checking up on me, Dr McIntyre?'

'Just making sure you hadn't bitten off more than you could chew.' He straightened up. 'I can see I shouldn't have bothered.' His slow smile reached out and enveloped her, then he turned and left the hut.

Alex stayed with Murdoch until the big logger's breathing eased, then made her way back to the mess hall. Andrew was slowly working his way through a queue of patients and appeared not to notice her return. Alex slipped into her seat and waited for the next sore throat or sprained ankle.

By the time they had finished she was dog-tired and she was wondering how Andrew had been able to cope with the load on his own. When she took over Brawton she would start the clinic earlier, she resolved. Her workload back in town was not going to be as great as Andrew's.

They left the hall, now filling with loggers ready for their evening meal, and made their way to the Land Rover through the gathering dusk. Still silence between them, but it was a comfortable, tired silence. Alex slipped back against the passenger seat and closed her eyes. The Land Rover swung out on to the dark mountain road and she fell asleep.

She was awakened rudely as the Land Rover's brakes were jammed on. Andrew was spinning the wheel, fighting for control. The wheels skidded broadside, and Alex heard herself scream as the vehicle slid closer to the looming drop at the roadside. The Land Rover came to rest facing the way it had come, its wheels in the gravel only inches from the edge.

The passenger side was away from the drop. Alex climbed out, with Andrew clambering over the seats after her. They stood on the road and looked at the vehicle. Another few inches and it would have slipped over the side, a drop which seemed to go on forever. Lumbering placidly along the road, unaware of the drama it had caused, was a large, very fat wombat. Alex started to laugh. Every nerve in her body was on edge. She was shaking, with tears running down her face, but still the laughter came.

'Stop it!'

Alex caught at herself. Her hands came up to her face, trying to find some sort of control. Andrew reached out for her hands and pulled them away. Very gently, almost as if he was afraid, he pulled her into his arms. She clung there, her head buried in his shoulder. How long they stayed like that she couldn't tell. She was aware of her heart, pounding painfully and the warmth of his arms encircling her.

As if by mutual instinct they pulled apart. For a long moment they searched into each other's eyes. Alex gave a tiny gasp of pleasure before his mouth came down, seeking her lips. His hands went up and locked around the softness of her hair, pulling her to him. Her mouth responded, her body quivered against him. Behind them, the wombat disappeared unnoticed into the bush.

Headlights, boring through the night, pulled them apart. Alex stood dazed as men jumped from one of the logging trucks and came towards them with concern. She realised her hand was locked in Andrew's and tried to pull it away, but the grip tightened.

'Jeepers, Doc, what a place to do wheelies!' The men inspected the perilous position of the Land Rover with interest. 'Have you got parachutes fitted for this thing?'

Andrew laughed, but to Alex it sounded tight and forced. With a jolt she realised he was as shaken as she.

The men were competent and fast. With the edge of the road being wet and crumbling they judged it wasn't safe to get into the driver's seat and start the Land Rover, so they attached ropes and hauled it back on to the bitumen. Soon it was on its own side of the road, facing down the hill into the town. As they climbed back into the vehicle the men waved them off with more raucous laughter. 'Doctors make more money than stunt drivers, Doc. I'd give it up if I were you,' and,

'I'd try impressing her with your skill at Scrabble, Doc. I don't think this is going to exactly win the lady!'

Andrew gave them a wave and started slowly down the hill.

'Andrew?' Alex's voice was tentative.

Andrew stared straight ahead, his fingers clenched on the steering-wheel.

'I'm sorry.' His voice was curt.

'It wasn't your fault.'

He glanced briefly across at her and then back to the road. 'I said I'm sorry.'

Did he mean the kiss or the accident? Sorry for what? Alex

was left with silence. His look forbade further talk.

As they drove into the hospital grounds, the main door opened and Margaret came out to meet them.

'Where have you been?' Her question was asked solely of Andrew. 'I rang the camp and they said you left an hour ago.'

He was reaching into the back for his bag.

'Sorry, Margaret. We had a slight accident.'

'An accident?' Her hand came out and held Andrew's arm. 'Darling, are you all right?'

He shrugged her off with a gesture of annoyance. 'We're fine. Just introduced Alex to the wildlife first-hand.'

Margaret cast Alex a look of incomprehension, then clearly decided it wasn't worth pursing.

'You have the board meeting tonight,' she reminded him gently. 'I've kept a dinner hot for you in my flat.'

'And Alex?'

Margaret smiled sweetly at Alex. 'I'm sorry, Alex, I didn't think of you. You do have your own kitchenette, you know.'

'Margaret——!' Andrew's voice was sharp, but Alex interrupted him.

'That's fine, Andrew, really it is. All I want is a hot bath anyway.' She left them to each other's company and made her way to the sanctuary of her tiny apartment.

Her flat was warm and welcoming. Like an automaton she prepared herself a meal. Mrs Mac had stocked her cupboards and refrigerator well, but Alex settled for soup and toast. She felt better when she had eaten, but the sense of unreality didn't fade. She started the bath, and while she waited for it to run she crossed to her still unpacked suitcases to start putting clothes away. In the folds of her sweaters she unwrapped a framed photo, a laughing Chris holding Timmy high in the air. She stood silently, looking down at the familiar faces.

Chris. He had been Alex's first love. She was studious, intense, and he whirled her into a vortex she had no control over. She loved him. She couldn't believe he loved someone as ordinary as she. Like a moth attracted by a bright flame she felt mesmerised. He filled her life with noise and love and laughter, and she would have followed him to the ends of the earth. He expected her to. Her protests that she should finish medicine were treated with derision. Her books were thrown aside and she followed him.

He was a pilot, running charter flights throughout Northern Australia. They lived a nomadic existence. Alex's hope of a settled home were ridiculed. If she stayed in one place, she would stay alone. Even when Timmy arrived there was only one way to be with Chris, and that was to be in the air, flying from one obscure settlement to the next. Alex had grown increasingly disenchanted with the life, but still Chris had held her mesmerised. She shook her head sadly as she gazed at the two laughing faces in the picture. For a while her life had been out of control. She couldn't allow it to happen again. No Dr Andrew McIntyre, for all his good looks and gentle smile, was going to infringe on her independence.

She held her fingers up to her lips and, unheralded, the thought of Andrew's lips against hers filled her thoughts. For a moment she let the memory catch and hold her, warm and reassuring. Then she looked down at the photo in its simple frame. She pushed the photo back into the now empty suitcase and thrust it on to the top of the wardrobe. The years of love and loss were over. The part of her indulging in the thought of a big, fair man with crinkly eyes was put firmly in its place. Dr Alex Donell, independent career woman, hopped into the bath.

CHAPTER FOUR

JANET came to wake her up the next morning, bearing coffee but no eggs and bacon.

'I'd hate you to think we were indulging you,' she chuckled as she pulled the blinds.

'What time is it?' Alex groped for her watch under the pillow.

'Quarter to seven and high time you were up. Actually,' Janet plonked herself down on the bed, 'you don't have to get up for a while yet, but I've done my morning chores and I was dying to see how you were getting on before Her Highness comes on duty.'

'Oh, Janet,' Alex giggled, 'you shouldn't talk like that!'

'Oh, Alex,' Janet mimicked, 'don't tell me you don't already call her worse things than that behind her back!'

Alex grimaced and sat up, hugging her knees. 'Why doesn't she like me, do you know?'

Janet grinned. 'Don't be blind, Alex Donell. The lady is jealous. Yes,' she went on as Alex shook her head, 'green as a rather nasty species of grass snake.'

'Oh, Janet, don't!' Alex protested weakly.

'It's true,' Janet said vehemently. 'She has her sights set solidly on one Dr McIntyre, and for a while there before you came it looked as if she'd get him. You should have seen her last night when you were late! We were all treading very warily indeed, I can tell you.'

'That's ridiculous!' The thought of what they had indeed been doing on the road brought a blush to Alex's cheeks. 'I've got better things to do with my life than compete with Margaret Nash for the attentions of a man, especially one as prejudiced and conceited as Andrew McIntyre!'

Janet looked at her curiously. 'Well,' she said frankly, 'if I found him looking in my direction I'd have trouble facing the other way, I can tell you.'

'I thought you had a boyfriend,' Alex reiterated. 'Charlie Taylor told me. . .'

'Charlie!' Janet exploded. 'Is there nothing that man doesn't know? He comes into the valley every six months and he manages to catch up on all the gossip in the space of the first half hour! He must be a fantastic auditor. If anyone were to start cheating the bank tomorrow he'd have heard about it yesterday! Yes,' she continued morosely, 'I've got a boyfriend, and a very nice boyfriend he is too, but—well, if he can look at pin-ups of Raquel Welch I can keep the odd soft spot for Andrew McIntyre. With those blue eyes . . . It's not fair on us women to give men eyes like that!'

'Janet Davis, this is not respectable talk at seven o'clock in the morning!' laughed Alex.

'Yes, well, who's talking of respectable?'

Alex followed Janet's line of vision and looked down at herself. Her pale pink négligé plunged downward, leaving little to the imagination. Chris had loved gorgeous nightwear and Alex took pleasure in choosing pretty things. Some quirk in her nature, she guessed.

'Wasted,' Janet went on. 'Couldn't you summon up just a little bit of interest in him? I'd so like someone nice to humanise him. When he's not around her he's really very nice.'

'Not even for you,' Alex laughed.

'Is there someone else?'

Twenty-four hours before Alex would have cringed at the question. Now she didn't seem to mind. 'No.' She followed Janet's gaze to the white mark on her ring finger. 'Not any more.'

A look of pain must have crossed her face fleetingly, and Janet was a sensitive girl.

'I'm sorry, Alex, I didn't mean to pry. I just open my mouth to put my foot in it!' She rose and spoke to herself severely. 'Not another word, Sister Davis, and no more questions.' She walked resolutely to the door, opened it and went out. The door had almost shut behind her when it swung open again and her face peeped around. 'Though if you ever want to tell me, I'm a very good listener.' She gave a cheeky grin and disappeared.

Alex settled back against the pillows to enjoy her coffee. A knock echoed through the flat.

'Come in!' she called.

She expected Janet to bob through the door again, but Andrew appeared instead. She clutched her négligé self-consciously, spilling some of her coffee in the process. He stood in the doorway, his frown deepening every moment.

'Can I help you?' asked Alex.

'Aren't you fussy who you let into the flat?' he demanded. 'I could have been anyone!'

Alex flushed. 'You weren't. You were you,' she said irrationally. 'I thought . . .' She held the folds of her flimsy nightwear closer, trying to control her mounting colour. 'What do you want?' she rounded on him, abandoning attempts at explanations. It wasn't any of his business what she thought. Damn the man, she was behaving like a schoolgirl!

His face was impassive. 'I'm needed up at Kinley again

this morning. There's a couple of blokes up there who really should be in hospital, but I don't want to put them through the trip down here. If you can hold the fort here I'd be grateful.'

He looked anything but grateful. Alex gazed up at him in incomprehension. Yesterday's interlude might just as well never have happened.

'Certainly. I'm sure I can cope here.' It was impossible to achieve the dignity of a competent career woman when he was towering over her and she was dressed in pink fluff. She made a mental resolve to buy a pair of pin-striped flannel pyjamas with buttons that did up to the throat.

She wished he would go away. Her discomfiture increased by the minute.

'Last night . . .' Andrew stopped.

Alex didn't help him. She couldn't.

He ran his hand through his hair, a gesture Alex was coming to know. 'Today's Wednesday. If it stays fairly quiet down here for the next couple of days we might be able to take Sunday off. Have you done any bushwalking?'

'Heaps,' lied Alex.

'The Kinnon Falls are about an hour's drive and a good couple of hours' walk from here, but they're magnificent.' He glowered at her. 'You'd appreciate them.'

Yes, sir, if you say so, sir, thought Alex rebelliously, but heard herself calmly agreeing with him. What on earth was she doing?

Another awkward silence fell. For a few moments Andrew stood looking down at her pink frivolity, then he wheeled out of the room.

Alex was left with a cold cup of coffee and an unwelcome sensation that today would be empty without him.

'Drat, drat and double drat!' She bounced out of bed and headed for the shower.

The next few days were busy as Alex got to know the hospital routine. Her relationship with Margaret remained strained, but Alex found that by remaining rigidly formal they could work side by side. Andrew she saw very little of. The medical work was more than enough for two doctors, and she quickly realised she would have very little time for socialising. That was the way she wanted it, however, and as the week drew to a close she found she was more contented than she'd imagined she could have been. The demons that had troubled her for years were slipping away in this remote spot with its constant demands on her. Perhaps she just didn't have enough time to think. Certainly at night when she hit the pillow there was no energy left for restless nights or bad dreams.

On Friday she took an hour off at lunchtime and bade farewell to Charlie.

'It's going to work out, I think,' she confided to him. 'I know it's early yet, but there's plenty of work, and I think I can cope.'

'And with Dr McIntyre and Matron Nash?' His eyes twinkled at her.

'Problems, I agree,' admitted Alex. 'The high-and-mighty Dr McIntyre might just have to eat a few words before we settle down to a good working relationship.' She laughed.

'And Matron?'

Alex looked worried. 'I honestly don't know, Charlie. For some reason she's got it in the gun for me.'

'The hospital's too small for both of you?'

'It might boil down to that,' Alex admitted, 'but I hope not. I'm working on it.' She rose from the table where they had been having lunch and impulsively leaned down and kissed his cheek. His ruddy complexion deepened. 'Thank you, Charlie.'

He caught her hand. 'I've done nothing. I wish you all the luck in the world.' He hesitated. 'Alex . . .'

'Yes?'

'Those ghosts you're carrying around—I hope you lay them.'

Alex looked down at him, disturbed. The man saw too much. She was glad he was a friend.

'I hoped they weren't that obvious,' she said ruefully.

'They're not. I've got second sight.'

'So I've been told. Come back soon, Charlie.'

She left him and walked the mile or so back to the hospital. She would miss him.

She had to take another hour off on Saturday and she needed Janet. When she confided her problem Janet went into whoops.

'He's asked you to go with him? I would kill to see Matron's face when she finds out!'

Alex grew serious. 'Janet, it really is silly. If it's going to cause any ill feeling perhaps I shouldn't go.'

'Not go? Don't be daft, Alex Donell! You're going to go if I have to get behind you and push!'

Alex smiled, but she remained worried. 'Honestly, Janet, it's not important enough to cause a rift over. It's not as if I'm interested in him.'

'I don't believe you. No girl could possibly be uninterested in a hunk like that, and if you're still pining over a lost love,' Janet held Alex's hand up and indicated the white mark, 'a little romance is just what the doctor ordered.'

'Yes, ma'am,' Alex responded meekly.

'And now,' Janet continued, 'what is the problem?'

'I told a whopper. I've never bushwalked in my life.'

Janet gazed at her speculatively, laughter lurking behind her eyes. 'So we have twenty-four hours to turn you into a bushwalker. It can't be done.'

'Why not?'

'How much does the stem of a toothbrush weigh?'

'I haven't a clue!'

'Well, there you are, then. What's scroggin?'

'It sounds fearsome. Whatever it is I won't do it.'

Janet burst into delighted laughter. 'We've got twenty-four hours' intensive training to do, Dr Donell.'

'Can you take me in hand?' asked Alex.

'Certainly, my dear.' Janet assumed an expression of worldly wisdom. 'Anything you need to know about bushwalking, just ask me. Pirrengurra is a base for serious bushwalkers, and I've nursed scores of them, suffering from anything from sunburn to gastro from all their foul dehydrated food. You can pick the fanatics. You unpack their toiletries, and their toothbrush is chopped off at the stub to save weight.'

'And scroggin?'

'Scroggin is a weird mix of anything edible, especially formulated to give them energy. It contains a large percentage of chocolate and sultanas as well as lots of unrecognisable little delicacies all mushed up together. It generally manages to pervade their entire backpack. You get little bits of glued-on chocolate everywhere.'

'I don't think I'm going to make a very good bushwalker,' sighed Alex.

'Nonsense! Where's your determination, woman? First things first, though. You need gear. There's a bush-gear outfitters in the main street. Bushwalking's our main tourist drawcard here, so they're well catered for as a breed.'

The two girls headed for town, roaring down the main street in Alex's deafening vehicle. Janet blocked her ears in disbelief.

'I like turning heads, but this is ridiculous!' she laughed.

The shop had everything Alex could possibly need, and Janet had a whale of a time. Alex purchased a big japara jacket—compulsory, Janet explained—and thick socks. The heavy moleskin trousers she felt she could do without, as she did the enormous hiking boots brought out for her inspection.

'Give it a break,' she protested, laughing. 'I couldn't lift my feet in those, much less walk!'

In the end she settled for a light pair of leather boots—'not for serious walking', according to the disapproving assistant—but all she thought she could cope with. On the spur of the moment she bought herself a light day pack.

'It's not that I don't think these boots will be OK,' she pacified her two helpers, 'it's just that I can carry a pair of sneakers as insurance.'

'Sneakers? In the bush?' The man was genuinely horrified.

Janet was at the back of the shop, holding up a small calico bag with a drawstring threaded through.

'You'll need this for your scroggin, Alex.'

Laughing, they left the shop. The scroggin bag stayed where it was.

Sunday dawned ice-cold but fine. Alex was awake early. She was aware of a tingle of anticipation and repressed it fiercely. She did a hurried ward round. The hospital was quiet; there seemed no reason why they couldn't go. She went back into her flat and changed into her gear. Her reflection gazed back at her and she grinned. She almost looked genuine! On the spur of the moment she reached up and loosened the band that held back her chestnut curls. They fell, thick and luxuriant, on to her shoulders.She gazed again in the mirror and angrily pulled her hair back into place. The band was reapplied and she pinned it up severely. What was she trying to prove? she asked herself.

At ten a knock sounded on the door, and Alex opened it to Andrew. He eyed her speculatively, a gleam of humour lurking behind his eyes. Alex ignored it and swept out.

In the car park Andrew loaded a small pack into his Land Rover.

'Lunch,' he explained.

They were just climbing into the vehicle as Margaret's little white Porsche swung in beside them.

'Whoops,' said Andrew. 'Caught!' He climbed out again to greet her.

'Where are you two off to?' Margaret's tone was pleasant, but her eyes were calculating.

'Playing truant, please, miss.' Andrew assumed the expression of a naughty schoolboy caught in the act. In spite of herself, Margaret laughed.

'Going into the mountains? Well, heaven knows you deserve a day off.' Her gaze flicked past him into the interior of the Land Rover. Still pleasantly, she continued, 'I would have thought Dr Donell would still be nice and rested. It hasn't exactly been a hard week.' She turned back to Andrew. 'I thought the idea of another doctor was so you could take a break and someone else could deal with the emergencies.'

'Ah, but there aren't going to be any emergencies today, are there, Alex?' Andrew swung his long legs back into the driver's seat. 'It's a great day, the men aren't working, there's no football for the usual batch of broken noses and no babies due.' He reached into the car and produced a walkie-talkie. 'If anything dire does happen I can be reached on this—I'll carry it in my pack. We'll just have to break a few speed limits on the way home——'

'Andrew, perhaps she's right,' Alex broke in. 'I really didn't think. I should stay.'

'Nonsense!' Andrew's tone was irritated. 'Margaret can cope in the first instance with emergencies. We've been doing this when I've had to be away for the past two months. One more day won't hurt.' He looked up at Margaret and flashed her his heart-turning smile. 'I'm just sorry we can't invite you too, but Janet's off duty and one of us should be here. I really think Alex should get some sort of feel for the mountains before she's been here much longer.'

Margaret relented. If anyone smiled at me like that I'd relent too, thought Alex.

'Of course, darling.' Andrew gestured in irritation at the endearment, but she appeared not to notice. 'You're right, I'm worrying about nothing.'

She gave him her loveliest smile and stepped back to allow the Land Rover room to manoeuvre out of the car park.

Smart lady, thought Alex.

The drive through the hills was relaxed. It seemed as if once the decision had been reached to go they were both determined to enjoy themselves. Alex pushed away the thought of emergencies in the valley and soaked in the scenery. She took it in as she hadn't on the drive up to Brawton. They talked of the valley, the people and its troubles — at least, Andrew talked and Alex listened. His voice was nice, she thought, soft and resonant. The winter sun was warm through the windscreen. She felt a strange mixture of peace and happiness flow through her, a feeling she hadn't known for a long time.

They parked the car in a gravel cutting excavated from the hillside. A narrow walking track led away from the car park into the bush, with a dilapidated sign pointing optimistically along it: 'Kinnon Falls 1 hr'.

'I thought you said it took two hours to get there?' she queried.

'The sign assumes that you're fit,' Andrew told her.

Alex bridled. 'There's nothing wrong with me, Dr McIntyre.' She pulled her day pack over her shoulders. 'Shall we go?' She headed off down the track without waiting to see if he would follow.

It was ten minutes before he caught her up. He'd had to organise his gear and lock the vehicle, and Alex hadn't wasted any time. By the time he caught her she was beginning to suspect there might be something in what he had said. Her years of study had left her very little time for hard physical exercise. She ignored him as he came up behind her, however, and lengthened her stride.

'Alex!'

'What's the matter? Can't you keep up?' She had trouble keeping her breath even as she spoke.

She sensed rather than saw him grinning behind her and gritted her teeth. Of all the obnoxious, arrogant males! She thrust her nose in the air, her toe hit a tree root and she stumbled.

Andrew caught her before she fell. The grin grew wider. With fury she shrugged off the arm.

'Thank you, I can manage.'

'I'm sure you can.'

She looked at him suspiciously, but his eyes held admiration.

'Alex, I have to admit you're a very competent woman,' he said. 'I was wrong to say that a woman doctor was useless here. You're proving to be of enormous help.'

Alex glared at him.

'What more do I have to say?' he sighed.

'You can stop laughing when you say it.'

'Alex!'

She wheeled around to face him.

'Humph!' she snapped.

'Well, that's telling me, isn't it.' Andrew said drily.

She smiled, then caught the expression in his eyes and gave a gasp. She wheeled back to the path and kept walking.

'Alex?'

'What?'

His voice was meek. 'Would you mind slowing down just a little bit? I'm a bit puffed.'

Alex giggled and slowed down.

The rest of the walk was done in companionable silence. Alex found she was enjoying herself, enjoying the physical exertion and the feel of the cold, clean air in her lungs. She found a rhythm in the walking that left her mind free to think of other things. Andrew kept pace behind her, seeming to realise that the walking and the silence were filling a need in her.

It came as a shock when they came upon the falls. The path dropped suddenly on to a ledge forming a natural look-out, and there below them was the river valley. They could see the falls sending up clouds of mist into the still air. The muted sound of the water echoed softly about them.

'Shall we go down?' Alex asked delightedly.

'Don't forget we have to come up again,' Andrew warned, but she was already starting down the path.

The sound of the water grew louder as they went. The path became claggy and wet and Alex slipped a couple of times. Always a hand reached out to steady and right her. She knew she should reject it, but a sneaking knowledge came over her that she liked it. By the time they reached the bottom the water was making a roar that prevented any attempt at conversation. They were at the very foot of the falls. The water was cascading down from a hundred feet above, crashing into the foaming mass of water at their feet. The spray soaked their faces and ran down their coats, and Alex gazed at it in stupefaction. It took her breath away.

In delight she turned back to Andrew.

'It's magnificent!' she yelled.

He was looking at her.

'What?'

She leaned closer.

'It's magnificent!'

'Sorry?'

She put her face close to his and he reached for her hands.

'It's mag——'

His face came down on to hers and took the last of her sentence to himself. His lips met hers, roughly pulling her up to meet him.

Alex gasped. His mouth imprisoned her lips, his hands moved to grasp her body, lifting her up. The mist on the falls settled on their faces, flowing down their foreheads and joining with their lips. Alex found herself responding with a fire she had not known her body possessed. Every nerve in her body awoke to him, pulling her closer, nearer.

They came apart slowly, like two people in a dream. Andrew placed his hands on her face, tracing the course of the water with his finger. Alex's body felt as thought it no longer belonged to her. She shook her head numbly.

'Andrew, no!'

'What do you mean, my love?' He bent down gently to hear her. 'Alex, yes.'

He took her mouth again, his tongue tracing the outlines of her teeth. His hands moved through the opening of her jacket, feeling the tautness of her breasts through her sweater. They moved gently down, holding her body hard against himself. She was aware of his arousal. Her body woke to it, responding with its own flame of desire.

This time it was she who pulled away. She shook her head as Andrew reached for her again. She was aware that she was crying, the tears mingling with the mist on her face. Blindly she pushed away and started climbing the steep slope up from the falls. Andrew stayed where he was for a moment, watching her go. When she had climbed for perhaps three minutes he started up the track after her.

By the time Alex reached the look-out she had herself under control and was able to turn and greet Andrew with a wavery smile.

'They told me bushwalking is a hazardous sport, and now I know why!' she said breathlessly.

Andrew looked down at her, concern in his eyes.

'Alex, what's wrong?'

She looked down at her fingers. 'Let's leave it, shall we?' She looked up again beseechingly. 'Please?'

He looked at her for a long moment. Silence hung in the air between them. He smiled reassuringly into her eyes.

'OK, my lovely. Let's have some lunch.'

From the depths of his pack he produced a groundsheet which he spread on the flat of the path.

'I don't exactly think it's going to get trampled,' he

grinned. 'The pedestrian traffic isn't what you might call heavy at this time of year.'

Another forage into his pack and lunch appeared—mouth-watering club sandwiches, with cucumber, curried egg, smoked ham and salmon, all garnished with tiny sprigs of parsley. Cold parcels of chicken, wrapped in lettuce with a delicate lemon mayonnaise spread through. Bite-size chocolate éclairs and melt-in-the-mouth lamingtons that must have only been finished that morning. Huge red apples, 'the pride of the island,' said Andrew, and to top it off a bottle of Moselle with two crystal wine glasses.

Alex burst into delighted laughter.

'You've obviously got some hold over Mrs Mac! Janet promised me dehydrated beef stew. I'm disappointed, Dr McIntyre.'

His face fell ludicrously.

'I'm so sorry.' He fished in the bottom of his battered pack and unearthed a grubby calico bag. 'I can offer you some scroggin, though.' He handed it to her triumphantly.

The tension broke and they attacked their meal with relish.

'Tell me about you,' begged Alex. 'Why are you here?'

'Here this minute?' He smiled at her and she broke in hurriedly,

'I mean in this valley. How long have you been here?'

'About four years.'

'And what makes you stay?'

Andrew leaned back with a sigh against an outcrop of rock. He absently polished an apple on his sweater and paused to admire its gleaming redness before gesturing to the wilderness before them. The apple swung in a wide arc.

'This,' he said simply. 'This place calls to me and holds me as nowhere else in the world can do. I came here after a stint as a GP in a wealthy city suburb. The shock hasn't left me.' He paused and bit into his apple reflectively. 'Here I can practise the sort of medicine I like. The people need and appreciate me. I've got a great little hospital with magnificent staff. What more could a man ask for?'

'Except you've got too much work to do.'

He looked down at his apple, seemingly intent on the white gash bitten out of the red. 'Did have,' he corrected. 'There was something missing, I'll admit.' He looked up at her, his voice softening. 'Not any more.'

Alex blushed.

'Just a woman, though,' she reminded him severely.

'There is that,' he said, his eyes crinkling at the corners. 'There is that.'

Silence. Alex fought her crimson cheeks and started packing wrappers back into containers. Andrew watched her.

'And you?' he asked.

'What?'

'This isn't fair, Alex Donell! I've told you my all. Now it's your turn.'

Alex looked up at him, hesitating.

'There really isn't much to tell.'

'Why are you here?' he wanted to know.

'For much the same reasons as you, I guess.'

'Liar.' He said it without rancour.

Alex gazed at him, not knowing what to say. He dumped his apple core in the box of refuse and reached forward. Lifting her left hand, he placed his finger on the white mark where the ring had been.

'I was right, wasn't I? There was someone else?'

'Yes.'

There was stillness between them. Andrew lightly held her

fingers, a question in his eyes. Alex withdrew her hand and pulled herself back out of his reach. She hugged her knees.

'Chris. My husband.' Then, at the look on his face, the rest came out in a rush.

'They were killed in a plane crash six years ago.'

'They?'

'Chris and Timmy. Our little boy.'

'Oh, my dear!'

He reached out for her, but Alex drew back, her eyes not leaving his face.

Silence. Andrew closed his eyes and sighed.

'For one insensitive idiot I really take the cake! I can't believe the things I said to you.'

'It doesn't matter,' she said quietly.

'It does.'

'No. It was a long time ago.'

Another long silence. High above them, a hawk wheeled across the sky on the high air currents.

'Was it a good marriage?' Andrew asked.

'No!' Alex surprised herself with her response. Anger welled in her, anger that had been suppressed for too long. 'It was an awful marriage. Oh, I loved him — you can't believe how I loved him. And Chris — well, Chris loved life. If anything was happening he had to be in the middle of it. Timmy and I were out there on the edge somewhere, a place to come home when he needed to recharge his batteries ready for the next big adventure. The night Timmy was born someone rang asking him to drop supplies to a camel train somewhere in the Northern Territory. He got me a taxi to the hospital. If Timmy and I could fit in with whatever he was doing our marriage was fine. The minute we were a nuisance there wasn't any marriage at all.' She stopped and then continued, her voice still full of pain. 'Anyway, as I said, it's all behind me. I was so young.' She looked at Andrew, his face still and watchful.

'I've carefully built myself a life, and it's a good life. I'm a doctor and I intend to become a damn good one. I'm on my own, and I'm happy to stay that way.' She glared defiantly across to Andrew.

'And along comes Andrew McIntyre, disturbing your careful plans.'

'You're not disturbing me at all,' she assured him.

'Alex, you have this nasty habit of telling fibs!'

She glared at him.

'Alex,' his voice was infinitely gentle, 'I won't hurt you.'

Alex's eyes welled with tears. Furiously she started shoving things back into the packs. She couldn't look at him.

'Please, Andrew,' she muttered. 'Let's go home.'

The walk back took forever. Alex was tired and tense, aware every moment of the man walking steadily behind her. Her feet hurt, but somehow it merged into a much deeper pain. The countryside blurred into a sea of green. She concentrated on keeping one foot in front of another. When Andrew called a halt, they had perhaps another three quarters of an hour's walk to do.

'You're not going to make it, little one,' he told her gently.

No one had ever called Alex 'little one' before. She turned it over in her mind and shook her head. She kept on walking.

'Alex, this is stupid! You're going to trip and hurt yourself in a minute. You're walking like a robot.'

'I can manage.'

'Alex!' He lengthened stride, caught up and swung her round to face him. 'Sit!'

She made to push him away, but the hands were firm. She

was pushed back on to a fallen tree trunk and sat there, passive. Andrew looked at her closely.

'Either you're more upset than I give you credit for or there's something wrong. Take your boots off.'

'I beg your pardon?'

'You heard me, woman. Take your boots off.'

Alex opened her mouth to argue and thought better of it. She didn't have the strength left for a fight. She hauled the boots off and gazed with detached interest at her feet.

They were a mess. A mass of blisters had burst, leaving ragged, raw wounds on both her heels. Both feet looked swollen and angry.

'When did you buy those boots?' Andrew's voice was hard.

'Yesterday morning.'

'Yesterday morning?' His exasperation was barely held in check. 'You bought boots for a long walk the day before you came? You've got rocks in your head! I suppose you didn't even think to pack a spare pair of boots in case these hurt?'

'I did.' Alex's voice was defensive.

'Well, where the hell are they? Why haven't you got them on your feet?'

Alex swung her day pack down. Without comment she unpacked her spare sneakers and put them on. Her feet screamed at being put back into shoes, but she ignored the pain and laced them up. She stood up. Andrew eyed her in disgust.

'How far do you think you'll get like that? I'll go ahead to the truck and bring back some dressings.'

'They won't make any difference,' she insisted.

'Then I'll have to carry you. For heaven's sake, you can't walk on those feet!'

Alex ignored him and started walking. Andrew's protests went unheeded and he was left to follow.

She didn't stop until she reached the truck. Wearily she climbed in and lay back against the seat. Her beautiful day was ruined. Why? Because this man did strange things to her heart that she didn't want to know about? He threatened her precious independence, shook the foundations of her fragile happiness.

He climbed in beside her. A large hand came out and traced the contour of her cheek.

'That was some effort, little one.'

She flinched. It would be so easy to give in to this man, to find haven in his strength. She had given in once before, though, and found where dependence could lead. She edged herself further from the driver's side and shut her eyes. She feigned sleep until the Land Rover pulled up outside the hospital.

As they pulled to a halt, she struggled with her seatbelt, avoiding Andrew's eyes. He leaned across and unclipped it for her and his hand brushed again across her cheek. The faint touch sent tremors running through her body. She looked up at him piteously and her fear must have come through, for he pushed her chin up and searched her face. His voice, when he spoke, was suddenly harsh.

'You're not to compare me, Alex, do you understand?' Almost to himself he added, 'I could kill the bastard!'

Alex shook her head mutely.

His hand held her face for a long moment, reading the misery in her eyes.

'I'm not known for my patience,' he warned, 'but I'll do my best not to rush you.'

He bent and gave her a feather kiss, brushing her lips

gently with his.

'Would you like me to put something on those feet?' In the dark, she could hear the smile in his voice.

'No, thank you,' she managed stiffly.

'Goodnight, then, Alex. Go in and get some sleep before I forget my resolution.'

Alex fled to the sanctuary of her little blue bedroom, but it was many hours before sleep overcame her. Her mind was in turmoil. Her carefully built independence lay in tatters around her. She tried to concentrate on the image of Chris, remembering the agony of countless nights on her own with no way of knowing where he was. She found that the image was blurring. Superimposing all her hurtful memories was a pair of gentle blue eyes which seemed as if they could see right to her heart.

CHAPTER FIVE

MONDAY morning saw Janet bouncing on the end of Alex's bed at six-thirty.

'Sorry, Alex, but I couldn't wait a moment longer. How did it go?' she asked.

Alex groaned and buried her head under her pillow.

'Oh, come on, Alex! It can't have been that bad?' Janet's voice was burning with curiosity.

For answer, Alex stuck two feet out from under the bedclothes. She deposited them unceremoniously on Janet's lap, then winced as the pain of the movement hit her. Janet eyed them with distaste, then let out a yelp of horror as the extent of the damage became apparent.

'Oh, Alex!'

'Oh, Janet!' Alex mimicked. 'I thought you said you knew all about bushwalking.'

'Well, I do,' wailed Janet. 'I know what bushwalkers do. I've just never done it.' She gazed down at the feet in dismay and then, in a tiny voice, ventured, 'Did you have to stop? Was he dreadfully angry?'

'He offered to carry me home.'

Janet's mouth dropped.

'Alex dear, are you kidding me?'

'No, I am not.' Alex swung herself crossly out of bed and tried to stand up. Her feet screamed in protest.

'The romance proceeds apace?' Janet's voice was tentative.

'No romance proceeds anywhere. Janet, I need sticking

plasters, and plenty of them.' Alex hobbled feebly to the bathroom.

A lesser mortal would stay in bed, she thought grimly, and then, suddenly, I want my mother. She pushed the thought aside. The week had begun.

It was a week of work in earnest, which was just as well for Alex's peace of mind. She hobbled from patient to patient, arousing amused sympathy as she went. Her encounters with Andrew were mercifully brief. As they passed he put his head down and made manly efforts to hide his laughter. At her first clinic on Monday morning a prescription form was left on her desk: one wheelchair to be loaned by the hospital for a period of one week, signed Andrew McIntyre. If it had been anyone but Andrew, Alex would have been delighted at the joke. As it was, she stared grimly at the note before crushing it and hurling it in her waste-paper basket. Why did he have to affect her this way?

Margaret eyed Alex's painful walk without sympathy.

She had difficulty in disguising her scorn. I'd like to see you in walking boots, thought Alex nastily, and grinned to herself at the thought of the immaculate Margaret in bush gear.

It was impossible to keep the reason for her limp to herself. The whole town seemed to know by nine o'clock on Monday morning. The men at Brawton loved it. When she went there for her clinic they were noisily solicitous.

'What's he been doing to you, Doc? I'd keep away from Andrew McIntyre if I were you. First he tries to drop you off a cliff and now he cripples you! There surely must be enough work for the two of you—he doesn't have to go to these lengths to get rid of a rival!'

Only the thought that Andrew would be getting as hard a

time as she was gave her any comfort at all.

She was settling into the job with ease and found herself looking forward to each clinic. As the winter deepened the casualties increased among the men in the logging camps. Equipment slipped, vehicles overturned, bronchitis and associated illnesses were commonplace. Alex treated their chilblains, sewed their cuts and listened to their worries, laughing with them and sympathising in turn. The men soon discovered she could give as good as she got and delighted in teasing her. She teased back and developed an easygoing friendship.

Mrs Mac and Janet made the job finding out patients' backgrounds simple. Between the two of them they seemed to know the life history of every resident of Pirrengurra and the surrounding logging camps, right down, it seemed to Alex, to what brand of socks they wore and what they'd eaten for breakfast that morning. Mealtimes with the pair were a constant source of amusement, and Alex felt she had found real friends.

Three days after the bushwalking episode Mrs Mac came to see her, sliding self-consciously into the waiting-room as the last patient left. Alex gestured her in with pleasure. This elderly lady, with her country cooking and kindly smile, had done a lot to make Alex feel welcome and at home.

She came in with some embarrassment and sat with her hands nervously clasping and unclasping, while Alex closed the door. Alex gave her a reassuring smile.

'What can I do for you, Mrs Mac?' She sat down behind the desk.

The lady looked distressed, consciously studying her hands.

'I'm not one to make a fuss,' she finally said in a small

voice. 'I hate bothering you. I never would Dr McIntyre—he's that busy. It's just, you being a lady and all, I thought—well, I thought you wouldn't mind if I came and saw you.'

'Of course I don't mind,' Alex said gently. 'And neither would Dr McIntyre. You're our friend as well as our patient and we're here to help.' She stood up and went round to the other side of the desk, perched on its edge and looked down. She realised tears were sliding slowly down the wrinkled face, and placed her fingers against a cheek. 'Tell me what the problem is.'

'It's something awful.'

'Just tell me.' Alex's voice was calm.

'I've got cancer.' Mrs Mac's voice broke and she buried her face in her hands.

'How do you know?'

Mrs Mac found her handkerchief and dissolved into it.

'Mrs Mac,' Alex said firmly, 'it's no use being upset until we're both sure. Tell me how you know.' She waited, and gradually the older woman pulled herself together.

She clasped her hand across her stomach. When she spoke her voice was little more than a whisper, and Alex had to lean close to her.

'At first I thought I was just getting fat. My tummy felt full—not swollen, just sort of uncomfortably full. I always have been big, a fine, strapping girl Bill used to say, and working in the kitchen all the time—well, I like my food. I suppose after a while I thought I'd better lose some weight, and really I haven't been feeling like eating much for a while. I guess that's what's made me so sure all of a sudden. My arms and legs are getting almost skinny, but when I looked in the mirror this morning I looked pregnant.' She looked fearfully up at Alex. 'Honest! If I wasn't over sixty with my Bill dead these past ten years I'd be sure I was in the family way.' She stopped and the clasping and unclasping of the hands began again. Her eyes didn't waver from Alex's.

Alex met her gaze, her outward calm belying the dismay she was feeling. She'd heard these symptoms before. She assisted Mrs Mac with undressing and helped her on to the couch. She knew even before she examined her what she would find, and it was there, a diffuse mass spreading through the abdomen.

'I'm right, aren't I?' The elderly lady's voice was tentative.

'Not necessarily. It could be a very large ovarian cyst.' Alex caught the work-worn hands and held them between her own. 'The first thing we do is find out. We need to do a laparotomy—that is, open up your tummy and take a look.'

'How do you do that?' Mrs Mac's voice rose fearfully. 'I don't want to go away from here.'

'You don't have to,' Alex reassured her. 'Dr McIntyre and I can operate here if you wish. We'll put you on our list for tomorrow morning, if that's OK with you.'

'So soon?'

'There's nothing to be gained by waiting.' She still held Mrs Mac's hands. 'There are three things we can find. Obviously there's what you're most afraid of, inoperable cancer. There's also a good chance that we're looking at a large, benign ovarian cyst, and you're probably not going to be too unhappy at losing the odd ovary now. Another alternative is that we could find a growth that we can excise—that is, remove completely. They're all possibilities.' She smiled softly. 'Don't order the shroud yet, OK?'

Mrs Mac gave a watery chuckle and pulled herself up from the couch.

'I wouldn't worry so much,' she admitted, 'if it wasn't for Tom.' She started to pull her dress back on. 'I suppose since Bill died I've accepted that it's got to come to me one day, and even though I wouldn't mind hanging on for a few years yet I'm not going to be bitter if it's not going to happen. I just dunno who'd look after Tom.'

'Tom?' queried Alex.

'My cat. At least, he's not really my cat. He just appeared at the hospital kitchen a couple of years ago and I've been looking after him ever since. Matron'd have a fit if she knew!'

Alex laughed.

'You mean the disgustingly fat black tomcat who washes his whiskers on my bedroom windowsill every morning? A sufferer if ever I saw one!'

'He is fat,' Mrs Mac agreed fondly. 'He depends on me, though. And who's going to do the hospital meals if you operate on me?'

'I'll look after Tom for however long you need me to,' Alex promised. 'And let Matron worry about the meals. She's bound to have people she can call on. Not that they could come up to your standard, though.'

By the time she had all the information she needed she had Mrs Mac almost cheerful. She saw her to the door, then went back to sit at her desk, her face creased in worry.

Andrew found her there when he returned from his clinic at Kinley. He came in quietly, closing the door behind him.

'What's up, Alex?' he asked.

Alex told him.

'I don't like it,' she admitted. 'I think we're going to find a mess tomorrow.'

'Why?'

'She's losing weight. And her skin—she hasn't noticed,

but when you look closely already there's a touch of jaundice.'

'Are you sure you're not reading things that aren't really there just because you're afraid for her?'

'I might be,' Alex admitted. 'I hope so. I'm too fond of her to be dispassionate.'

'The price we pay,' Andrew said softly. 'Come on.' He stood back to allow her to precede him out of the room, his fingers gently touching her arm as she passed. 'We need to do ward rounds. The best thing we can do is to keep busy until morning.'

The surgery scheduled for the following morning was minor: Joe Schelling's ingrown toenail, Mr Grant's hernia, and then Mrs Mac. Alex had elected to do the anaesthetic while Andrew operated. They both greeted her as Janet and another nurse wheeled her in.

'Eh, you look different,' she murmured sleepily. 'I wouldn't have known you.'

'It's just the same us under the masks,' Alex reassured her. She continued talking softly of inanities until the anaesthetic took hold, then concentrated on her job. Her attention moved from chest movement, to Mrs Mac's face, to the dials on the anaesthetic trolley, and she didn't allow herself to glance elsewhere. She blotted out what Andrew was likely to find.

There was silence in the little theatre. The two nurses were old friends of the lady on the table and both had enough intuition to realise the outcome could be serious. The usual chatty atmosphere of surgery was non-existent.

'Damn!'

Alex's eyes flew to Andrew's face, then as quickly back to the dials on the trolley.

'We're closing.' Andrew's voice was weary and defeated. 'Damn!' he repeated.

Alex bit her lip and said nothing. She had her job to do and she did it.

With Mrs Mac wheeled back to the ward Andrew and Alex were left alone. They cleaned up wordlessly, Alex wanting to ask but not wanting to hear the answer. Andrew finally broke the silence.

'There's nothing we can do, Alex. It's a massive tumour, stuck firmly to the abdomen wall and caught up in the bowel. There's obvious lymph node enlargement and visible secondaries in the liver.'

Alex drew in her breath and looked at him. Andrew concentrated on meticulously cleaning his hands, then straightened and reached for a towel. His eyes met hers in sympathy and concern.

'She's your patient, Alex. It's up to you now to keep her comfortable until the end. By the look of it, that's not going to be far away.'

Alex nodded and left the room.

When Mrs Mac woke Alex was sitting beside her, watching the branches of the giant gums creaking and swaying in the wind outside the ward window. She was deep in thought and only gradually became aware that the still figure in the bed was awake and watching her.

'It's cancer, isn't it?' Mrs Mac's voice was barely a whisper.

'Yes.'

'Inoperable?'

'Yes.'

'I thought so.' Mrs Mac sounded almost satisfied. The eyes

closed and she drifted off again into sleep.

Alex rose stiffly and left. As she came out into the corridor Andrew swung himself down from the ledge where he had been waiting. He said nothing, just stood and looked, a long, serious, questioning look. Alex's eyes filled with tears. Before she could help herself she had walked into the comfort of his arms, burying her head in his shoulder and finding the solace of a hurt child in his strength.

CHAPTER SIX

MRS MAC'S recovery from the operation was slow and, as her wound healed, the slight touch of jaundice Alex had noted at her first examination deepened. She accepted with stoicism the fact that she wouldn't be going home. The thing she found hardest was losing her normal sources of gossip, and Alex's ward rounds stretched to almost double to allow time for Mrs Mac's questioning. Often she found Andrew settled comfortably on the end of the bed when she arrived, and Janet was never far away. Mrs Mac was never happier than when she had the three of them there together.

'Haven't you any family?' Alex asked her.

'You're the only family I have,' she smiled at the three of them. 'I don't need anyone else.'

Between Andrew and Alex there was constraint. The scene outside Mrs Mac's door on the day of her operation would not be repeated, Alex resolved. There was not much Mrs Mac's eyes missed, though, and she pounced on this new morsel with delight.

'He's soft on you,' she told Alex gleefully.

'You're a nosy, interfering old baggage,' Alex told her crossly.

Mrs Mac's grin just broadened, and Alex made her escape.

The time Alex could spend worrying about Mrs Mac was limited. Her practice in town was building up to the point where she wondered how Andrew had ever coped on his own.

She enjoyed her hospital clinics. She found them different but just as rewarding as the medicine she practised in the logging camps. Among the tiny population of women she was welcomed with real pleasure, and she soon realised how isolated the women found the place. It was a man's world, and a woman in the doctor's surgery gave them an avenue to vent their frustrations at the restricted life they were leading. They sensed Alex's maturity and knew instinctively that her sympathy wasn't a pretence. Alex sometimes finished a morning's surgery feeling she had done nothing but listen, but she knew that, despite not curing any physical ills, she had done some good.

The town was starved of facilities where the women could meet. Alex cornered Janet as she was remaking Mrs Mac's bed and questioned her.

'Why isn't there a health centre in the town?' she asked curiously. 'Why do all the mums have to bring their children here to be checked?'

'The town's not big enough to warrant it,' Janet replied defensively.

'The town isn't, but if you include the logging camps it would have to be.'

'They're not permanent,' Janet objected.

'They mightn't be permanent, but they seem to have been here a mighty long time. Twenty years, isn't it? And I know their population is itinerant, but for every family that moves away another takes its place. It seems to me that the logging's not going to dry up in the next couple of years either.'

'I know that,' Janet grimaced. 'The problem is getting the rest of the town to accept that. They see the loggers as a nuisance that will one day disappear.'

'Well, it's time they stopped looking at them like that. They must realise that without logging this town would die. All the permanents depend on the camps for their trade. Even this hospital would have to close with only the tiny population of the town to support it.'

Janet looked doubtful, but Alex was firm.

'Look, a health centre is something we can easily set up, and at least it gives the young mums a place where they can meet each other.'

'What does Dr McIntyre think?' asked Janet.

'For heaven's sake, Janet, it doesn't matter what he thinks! It's a darned good idea.'

Janet shook her head, but gave a tiny smile.

'Good luck,' she said drily.

'What do you think, Mrs Mac?' asked Alex. Mrs Mac's eyes had been going from one to the other, her face alive with interest.

'It sounds a lovely idea. Don't you let her talk you out of it.' She shook her head reprovingly at Janet. 'I was that lonely when me and Bill first came here it doesn't bear thinking of. The townspeople wouldn't have a bar of us.'

'That settles it.'

Armed to the teeth with enthusiasm for a health centre, Alex turned her attention to finding a place to hold it. The local kindergarten was held four times a week and for the rest of the time the facilities lay idle. Alex approached the kindergarten directress and was met with a favourable reception. Once a week, she told Alex, they could convert the hall into a place where young mums could bring their children to be weighed and measured and have a cup of coffee while their offspring used the more indestructible of the kindergarten's facilities.

Delighted with the arrangement, Alex approached Matron. She needed Janet to run the centre. Could Margaret release her for three hours a week?

Thinking about it later, Alex realised she should have known better. The woman's dislike for Alex found vent in an icy refusal. Alex had caught her as they were cleaning up after Outpatients. Margaret didn't pause in her organisation of equipment for the next session.

'If you think I'm going to allow my staff time off to run a centre that the town doesn't need and doesn't want, you have another think coming——!' she snapped.

Alex broke in. 'Margaret——'

'Matron Nash.'

'I'm sorry. Matron, it's only for a trial period. We'll run it for four weeks and if no one uses it we've lost nothing.'

'Except I've lost four half-days' work from Sister Davis and the kindergarten has been put to all sorts of trouble. You can just put the idea back where it came from.'

Alex was stunned. She backed off and said mildly, 'Won't you even consider it?'

Margaret completed the tray of equipment she was laying out and turned to face Alex.

'Dr Donell,' the emphasis lay sardonically on the 'Dr', 'I have considered it for fully two minutes and that's two of my valuable minutes wasted. Now, if you'll excuse me, I have work to do.'

She opened the door and went out. Alex was left gazing uselessly after her.

'Told you so.'

'Janet!' Janet's cheeky grin appeared from an examination cubicle. 'You were eavesdropping!'

'Of course I was. How else is a girl ever going to learn anything?' She pushed the curtain back and perched on the end of the bed. 'You're going to have to do what you should have done in the first place.'

'Which is what?'

Alex knew the answer before she asked the question, but the reply came back just the same.

'Ask Dr McIntyre.'

Alex flushed. 'I really would like to set this up on my own,' she admitted.

'Well, you can't without Maggie's co-operation, and she's not going to give you that in a pink fit.'

'Why not?' Alex's tone was angry.

'Because she hates you,' Janet returned candidly. 'Ever since you arrived Dr McIntyre has been a changed person. He's actually been seen to laugh! Our serious Matron Nash does not like it one bit. To be frank with you, my dear, she's as jealous as hell.'

'Oh, for heaven's sake!' Alex spread her hands helplessly. 'Janet, what can I do?'

'Nothing.' Janet looked directly at her. 'There's nothing you can do to make the lady happy. Ask Dr McIntyre if you can have your health centre.'

'Janet, I don't want to!' Alex's voice was a wail.

'Do you want it or don't you?' Janet slid off the bed, straightened the covers and disappeared down the corridor.

Alex stood irresolutely. She was being stupid, she knew, but it had seemed important to make this one stance of being independent. The health centre was more important, though. She couldn't jeopardise it by reluctance to face Andrew. She looked at her watch. He should have just about finished his evening clinic. She squared her shoulders and marched down the corridor to knock forcefully on his door.

'Come in, Alex.'

She peered around the door. His eyes were watching her, grave with a hint of annoyance.

'How did you know it was me?' she asked.

'Margaret's just been in to see me. She's a bit upset.'

'She's upset?' Alex's voice rose in indignation.

'Alex, for heaven's sake, what is this?'

Andrew ran his hand wearily through his hair as she outlined her plans for the health centre. His eyes watched her and she faltered as she outlined her plans. As her voice trailed off, a silence fell. Damn, thought Alex. Why should I be feeling so miserable?

His voice, when he spoke, was edged with irritation.

'You never thought of consulting me or the hospital board first?'

'It wasn't worth it. You've got enough to worry about without this as well.' She didn't add her real reason, the desire to prove to him that she could implement a successful project without his assistance.

He shook his head.

'You've got a problem now, Alex. Maggie's worried about her staff. For all this place seems to be running like an efficient machine, Maggie's got a critical staff shortage. She just can't spare someone of Janet's calibre to spend half a day——'

'On some hare-brained project,' Alex finished for him.

'I didn't say that,' Andrew replied wearily. 'Look, Alex, I think it's a great idea, but we have to think about it. We'll have to get board approval so we can fund Janet's wages and we need to organise staff to cover her. If that can be done, well and good. If it can't, it can't. Meanwhile, leave it be. You've antagonised Maggie enough already.'

Alex stood and gazed down at him. Anger welled up in her, fury at this man sitting calmly in front of her. Her project, so carefully thought out and so obviously needed, was being shelved. Without a word she turned and walked out of the door. The echo of it slamming behind her resounded down the corridor.

She made her way back to the sanctuary of her flat. The late afternoon sun was streaming in at the window, making the kitchenette look warm and inviting. Alex made herself a cup of coffee and paced angrily. He was so damned supercilious! A tiny niggle at the back of her mind that he might be right only made her angrier. Unannounced, the memory of that weary gesture of his hand running through his hair came into her mind and stayed there. Through her anger she felt an overwhelming urge to return down the corridor and hold his fair head in her hands. In baffled frustration she slammed her coffee-cup down on the bench, slopping coffee over the laminex in the process, and left to do her evening ward round.

In the children's ward she found Rob, the little boy she had met on her first day in the valley, jumping on his bed in excitement, his plaster cast stuck out precariously in front of him. He greeted Alex with delight.

'Dr McIntyre says I can go home tomorrow!' His face was one huge grin.

Alex picked him up and whirled him round. He uttered a delighted shriek as she deposited him back on the bed.

'That's great news, Rob. We're going to miss you, though.'

'No, you won't. No, you won't!' His face was pink with excitement. 'Dad's playing in town on Saturday and Mum says we can all come, and I've already asked Dr McIntyre and he says yes he's coming — and you are coming, aren't you?' His voice was pleading but confident.

'Of course she's coming.' Andrew's voice from the doorway made Alex wheel around. 'We promised, didn't we,

Dr Donell?'

His voice was laughing, but his eyes gave her a definite message. Alex turned back to the little boy, his face anxiously watching them.

'I wouldn't miss it for quids,' she informed him. 'You'd better give me some tips beforehand, though. Who did you say your dad played for? Do you have team colours? I'd hate to barrack for the wrong team.'

In the face of such abysmal ignorance the two men looked expressively at each other.

'I'll leave you to educate Dr Donell, Rob,' said Andrew. 'I've got work to do.'

Half an hour later, after an intense education programme on the rules and customs surrounding Australian Rules football, Alex made her escape.

In the kitchen, Janet was finishing her dinner. Alex plonked herself down beside her and sighed with relief.

'What have I let myself in for?' she demanded, and outlined the last half-hour.

Janet was unsympathetic.

'Life here revolves around Saturday afternoon. I guess the sooner you get initiated the better.'

'Do you go?' asked Alex.

'Need you ask? My beloved plays for Kinley Firsts. What else should a devoted girlfriend do on a Saturday afternoon but watch the man in her life chase a little ball around in the mud? It's either that or sit at home and watch the league games on the television, and at least by watching the local games you've got a bit of an idea of what they're all talking about on Saturday night. Sometimes I'm lucky and have to work instead.'

Alex smiled absently, but her worry must have got through

to the other girl. She finished her coffee and looked seriously at Alex.

'Now, what's up?' asked Janet. 'Besides the fuss about the health centre, that is.'

'I have to go with Andrew.'

'Half your luck!'

'Janet, don't!' Alex twisted her hands on the table in front of her.

'You're serious, aren't you?' queried Janet. 'You really don't want to go?'

'I'd give heaps to get out of it,' Alex confessed.

Janet shook her head. 'I don't think you can, Alex. I really don't know why you should want to either, but I guess that's your business. I tell you what — would it help if we made it a foursome? Rob's dad plays for the reserves and they start at eleven. Con plays for the firsts and they start at two. If we all went early we could do both matches and you wouldn't be left alone with Dr McIntyre.'

'The whole day?' Alex was horrified.

'You're going to have to anyway. The locals would be insulted if you watched the reserves and went home before the main game. Besides which, Andrew likes to stay for the whole match. It's either watch the match and deal with casualties as they occur or spend the afternoon at the hospital waiting for them to come in.'

'Casualties?' queried Alex.

Janet grimaced.

'Mm. Heaven knows what they see in it — but then Con can't understand the attraction of netball. There's no fathoming the opposite sex.'

Alex spread her hands resignedly. 'OK, I know when I'm beaten. I'd be grateful if you would join us.'

'I'll enjoy it myself,' Janet admitted. 'Usually I have to stay with Con's mum and she nearly bursts my eardrums with her barracking, not to mention putting me to the blush with her abuse of the umpire! I'll organise it, and,' she went on as Alex tried to interrupt, 'I'll tell Dr McIntyre too. Why are you so afraid of going near the man, Alex Donell? He's really very nice.'

She rose from the table and left Alex to her own reflections.

Saturday was wet. Alex woke to hear drumming on the roof and squirmed back under the cover in delight. OK, Rob would be disappointed, but even he couldn't expect them to go in this downpour. She slept for an hour longer than usual, then did a leisurely ward round of the patients she had in hospital. As she checked Mrs Mac she was dismayed at her obvious deterioration. The jaundice was deeper and she was feeling uninclined to talk. As Alex completed her examination and wrote up her medication Janet appeared. She greeted Mrs Mac and levelled an accusing finger at Alex.

'Why aren't you ready?'

Alex gazed in horror at Janet's layers of woollens, gloves, cap and coat.

'You've got to be kidding,' she whispered.

An unsympathetic laugh was her answer.

'Come on, Dr Donell, where's your pioneering spirit? The boys are waiting in Con's car. Hurry up!'

Alex shook her head, bemused.

'This is ridiculous!' she protested.

'This is football.' Janet stamped her foot impatiently. 'Are you coming like that or are you going to move?'

'I'm moving — I'm moving!'

Mrs Mac's weak chuckle rang after them.

The hospital car park was a sea of mud as Alex reached it. Con owned a big Ford. He and Janet were in the front and Andrew had already settled himself into the rear seat. He smiled easily at her as she opened the rear door. Alex climbed self-consciously in and pushed herself into the corner as far from Andrew as she could reach. Con twisted around from the driving position to greet her, and Alex recognised another of the valley's big men. His huge frame filled the car. He grinned at her and she felt herself responding.

'You'd have to be a logger?'

'Not me, ma'am.' He shrugged his massive shoulders expressively. 'I leave that for the big guys. I'm an accountant at the local bank.'

'A pen-pusher in fact,' corroborated Janet. 'Weak as water.' She gave him a playful poke in the ribs and he retaliated by putting one arm around her and squeezing. Her light frame was lifted off the seat and up to be squeezed against him.

'Ouch!' Janet rubbed her shoulder with a grimace.

'No less than you deserve!' Alex caught their interchange of glances and realised that for all Janet's light-hearted banter about Andrew she was totally contented with her Con. She stole a look at Andrew and found him regarding her steadily. Blushing, she looked away. Con started the motor and they swished their way out of the car park.

Rob was waiting at the football ground gate, and as Con drew the car to a halt he greeted them with joy.

'You're late,' he said accusingly as he clambered aboard. His wet little body with the lump of plaster attached launched itself across Alex's and Andrew's legs. 'We've saved you a spot.' He tapped Con on the shoulder. 'Me dad's car is round the other side and I've got me mum stopping other cars pinching the spot next to it.'

'Yes, sir.' Con obligingly swung the car into position, hard against the fence bordering the oval. The reserves' match was already under way.

'There's me dad, there.' A grubby finger pointed imperiously to a figure in the centre of the ground. 'He's got two marks already.'

'Marks?' Alex's knee was soggy.

Rob was busy wriggling until he made himself comfortable on her lap. His muddy plaster cast he deposited carefully on Andrew's legs.

'A mark is when you catch the ball on the full.' His voice was scornful. 'Don't you know anything?'

Alex smiled apologetically. Her glance came around and caught Andrew's and the colour drained from her face. He was sitting watching her, and his expression held such tenderness it took her breath away. For a long moment their eyes held, then Rob's chatter forced their attention back to him. Alex felt suddenly sick.

Much to her relief, Rob stayed with them for the duration of the day. He gave Alex a shield she could use to separate herself from Andrew. When the rain eased a little and they were out of the car he hopped about them and narrated the game with gusto, leaving very little room for other conversation. When the rain came down in torrents and they stayed in the steamy confines of the car he bobbed up and down on Alex's knee, reaching over urgently to honk the horn on the odd occasions when Kinley scored a goal. In the third quarter his dad kicked a goal and his day was complete.

They ate a companionable lunch, pies with sauce munched out of paper bags and cups of piping hot coffee from the large thermos flasks Janet had packed. If only there weren't this tension between Andrew and herself Alex could have had a wonderful day. Not that it affected the others; they seemed unaware of her discomfiture and joked and cheered regardless. Alex was aware that the look of fatigue had slipped from Andrew's face. Obviously he liked Janet and Con; he and Con ragged each other mercilessly until it was time for Con to play.

'Watch out for the big boys,' he warned as Con collected his gear and hugged Janet goodbye.

'I don't have to today,' Con retorted. 'I've brought my own two personal physicians.'

'Well, I guess we'd enjoy working you over, wouldn't we, Alex? Make it something nice and gruesome.'

'Don't you dare!' Janet's voice was indignant. She looked up at Con with affection. 'Just win, sweetheart.'

'For you, anything.' He saluted and made his way to the changing-rooms.

The firsts' game was just as confusing as the reserves' to Alex. The ground was a mêlée of muddy bodies tearing after the ball. The game seemed like nothing as much as a glorious excuse for a mud bath.

Andrew was called out a couple of times during the match. It wasn't as dangerous a game as rugby, Janet assured her, but Alex wasn't convinced. She'd glanced into Andrew's bag that he'd prepared for the day and realised he'd come ready for anything from bruises to broken necks. The injuries for the day were relatively minor. One player streamed blood from a split forehead, and Alex was astounded to see him back on the field after Andrew had stitched him up. The other had a leg fracture. Andrew splinted his leg and he disappeared in the back of a utility, loudly bewailing his fate at being ordered to hospital.

'Don't we have to go and set it?' asked Alex.

'He wouldn't expect us to miss the game just for a broken leg,' Andrew grinned. He relented at the look on her face. 'It's not a bad break, Alex, honestly. Maggie'll do the X-rays and it can wait until this evening to be set.'

Con came back to them weary but triumphant at the end of the match, a great, sweaty, mud-coated figure. Rob greeted him with adulation. A firsts' player who was part of the winning team was obviously a man of the first order.

Janet was not quite so adoring.

'Get away from me, you great brute!' she ordered.

'Oh, Janet!' His voice was pathetic. 'Don't you love me any more?' Before she could defend herself he reached for her and embraced her with a bear's hug, leaving a large muddy kiss on her forehead.

Janet squealed in disgust and Andrew and Alex doubled up. Con let Janet down and eyed Alex dangerously.

'Is that any way to greet a conquering hero? Laughter? I expect adoration from all the wenches.'

Alex ducked behind Andrew and held on.

'Move, man,' ordered Con. 'You're keeping me from my due!'

Laughing, Andrew obliged. He reached back and held Alex's hands, then squatted, leaving her caught facing the huge muddy form in front of her. Con reached over and caught her face, planting a kiss firmly on her cheek. Alex touched her face. Rivulets of mud were streaming down where the fingers had held her. Weak with laughter, she turned on Andrew.

'Traitor!'

'Who are we to deny our hero the spoils of war?' He traced one of the trails of mud down her cheek. 'It suits you, I think.'

Alex choked. She and Janet retreated into the car to locate towels while Con disappeared to shower and change.

The team and spectators alike adjourned to the pub. Alex and Andrew were carried along in their wake and found themselves part of the Kinley celebration. From the other side of the bar abuse was hurled at them from the Pirrengurra team.

'This is lovely, this is! We'll have to fly to bloody Hobart to get our medical attention now. Two doctors in the town, and they're both on the same side!'

The atmosphere in the pub was warm and accepting, and Alex felt herself relax. She felt at home here, as though she had been part of the town for a long time. She sipped her shandy and sat back, enjoying the laughter, noise and gossip flowing over her, surrounded by people who already thought of her as a friend. When the call came through from the hospital telling Andrew the X-rays were ready she felt a strong pang of regret. Her eyes flew to his face and he smiled ruefully down at her.

'Never mind.' He touched her face lightly. 'I guess we've been lucky so far. We've had a whole day without a real interruption.' He turned to say goodbye to Con and Janet.

'We'll be seeing you next Saturday night at the finals' celebration though, won't we, Doc?' Con turned to Alex and explained, 'We have a big dance after the grand final. There's the odd speech thrown in, but we hurl things at speakers who go on for too long. It's a great night.'

'We'll be there, won't we, Alex?' Andrew's voice brooked no argument. He looked down into her face, a tiny smile hovering at the corners of his mouth.

'Fine,' Alex agreed weakly, her stomach sinking at the prospect. This man was dangerous.

Con threw Andrew the car keys.

'Janet and I will cadge a lift up to the hospital later and I'll collect the car then. Will you stay on with us, Alex?'

Alex rose also. 'No. Without wishing to give offence, I've had about enough football for one day. Thanks for a great time, though.'

She had enjoyed herself, she admitted to herself as she followed Andrew out to the car. These people were nice.

Andrew looked at her quizzically as he handed her into the front seat.

'Happy?' he queried.

'Yes,' replied Alex almost defensively. 'Yes, I am.'

He smiled at her but made no attempt to prolong their time together. As they pulled up outside the hospital he turned back to her.

'Seven-thirty next Saturday, then? Wear something pretty, Alex.'

He climbed out of the car and made his way briskly into Casualty. Alex was left gazing helpless after his retreating back.

Sunday was a quiet day for Alex. She did her ward round, missing Rob's cheerful chatter in the children's ward. Mrs Mac was drifting in and out of sleep. Alex sat with her for a while and told her of the previous day's events, but she wasn't sure how much was listened to or understood. Finally the sleep seemed to deepen and Alex came back to her flat. The place seemed lonely and quiet. Alex was used to spending most of her spare time alone and usually enjoyed the peace, so she was irritated with herself for wanting company. Tom, Mrs Mac's cat, was sunning himself on her window-ledge. She let him in and he gratefully settled himself on the rug in front of the gas heater. She washed her hair and settled down to write letters.

Her mind kept hovering over the next Saturday night. Wear something pretty, Andrew had said. Chauvinist, she muttered to herself, but it sounded trite even in her ears.

'I haven't got anything pretty!' she wailed. Six years of self-imposed exile had left her with a practical wardrobe containing nothing frivolous except her nighties. 'And I can't wear those,' she told the cat. His big yellow eyes gazed at her with interest.

'Do you suppose there's anywhere in this town where I can buy a dress?' she demanded. Tom was clearly uninitiated in the niceties of female fashion. Alex rubbed his shiny head. 'I suppose if I asked you where to go to buy cat food you'd tell me!'

Finally she crossed to the telephone and looked up Janet's number. Janet was home, by the sound of it having just the same kind of day as Alex.

'Con is having intensive training ready for next Saturday's final,' she told Alex disgustedly. 'What a waste of a Sunday off!'

She listened to Alex's problem with concern.

'Alex, there's nowhere in town to buy anything decent. Nothing of mine's going to fit you either — you've got six inches on me.' She paused. 'You'd be the same size as me, though. Can you sew?'

'Yes.'

'Me too.' Janet's voice was suddenly enthusiastic. 'Alex, I've got some gorgeous wool crêpe here. I bought it to make myself a long dress a couple of years back. It was a spur-of-the-moment purchase because I loved the colour — it's a really deep green — but in fact I've never made it because I know it'll make me look drab. With my mouse hair

I've got to wear bright colours, but green on you should look fabulous. There's enough fabric to make you a gorgeous cocktail-length frock, and I've got just the pattern——'

Alex broke in. 'Janet, I said I could sew, but I can't sew fast. It's lovely of you to offer, but I'd never do it in time.'

'No, but *we* could. Hold on to your hat, I'll be right over.'

Janet appeared at the flat door twenty minutes later, laden with gear. An inspection of the pattern and the material showed that it was possible. The dress was tightly fitted to the hips, with a high neck at the front and a plunging open back. At the hips, the skirt flared out in a full circle. The sleeves were long, with tiny buttons reaching to the elbows.

Alex sat back and considered it. 'It's gorgeous!' she exclaimed.

'Isn't it just? Designed for someone with your height, though. I don't know what came over me to think I could wear it myself. It's been sitting in my sewing cupboard for three years waiting for me to grow.' Janet picked the soft stuff of the material up and held it against her face. 'This material is dreamy! It cost me an arm and a leg. It's not everyone I'd be doing this for, Alex Donell,' she added.

'I'll pay you for it,' Alex said quickly.

'You don't know what you're saying. You'll have to approach the bank for a long-term loan, and on what security, may I ask?'

'I'll wear it in and wile my way into the manager's good graces.'

Laughing, the girls set to work. They worked well together, enjoying each other's company as well as the task in front of them. They broke for soup and crumpets at teatime, but by eight o'clock Alex was standing in front of the mirror gazing at herself in delight.

The dress clung to her figure, showing her trim proportions to perfection. The skirt shimmered and moved in the evening light. Alex turned gently around and the soft folds of the skirt swayed and resettled. The deep green highlighted the glowing chestnut of her hair. Janet reached up and loosened the knot at the back of Alex's head, and the curls fell dramatically, making the whole outfit seem romantically alluring. Janet gasped.

'Wow!'

Alex fingered the folds of the dress. She looked at Janet with a worried expression.

'Isn't it a bit — well, a bit . . .'

'Dressy?' Janet finished for her. 'Don't you believe it! This is the town's night of the year and they dress up to the nines. Have you got shoes?'

Alex produced elegant black court shoes with tiny heels. A pair of pearl earrings and the outfit was complete. Even the cat, who had supervised the entire operation from his vantage-point on the mat, seemed to regard her with approval. Janet packed up her gear with glee.

'Never let it be said that Janet Davis doesn't give her all for the cause of young love!'

'Janet!' Alex warned.

'I know, I know,' Janet laughed, and held up a hand defensively. 'You're just good friends. All I can say is that he'd be a strange man who could keep platonic thoughts in his head after seeing you like this!'

Alex was left by herself. She made a cup of coffee and sat stroking the cat's head reflectively. What was she doing? She had been steamrollered into attending this dance. What did it matter what she wore?

Because it matters very much what Andrew McIntyre

thinks of you, a tiny voice whispered in the back of her head.

She shook her head in disgust. There's no future in that, she told herself firmly. You've had your time of romance and disillusion. From here on in, Alex Donell, keep your feet firmly on the ground.

The sight of the green dress, hanging on the curtain rail, seemed to mock her. She prepared for bed, confused and disorientated. Her dreams that night were troubled — Andrew's face gently mocking as he watched a tall girl in a deep green dress swirl in the moonlight.

CHAPTER SEVEN

IT WAS just as well that Janet and Alex finished the dress on Sunday night. The following week turned out to be frantic, with every moment occupied. Alex ran the clinic at Brawton twice in the week, both sessions stretching well into the evening. Her Land Rover coped well with the mountain roads, but Alex was still tense after the episode with the wombat, and she returned to the hospital after each trip with a feeling of relief.

The hospital was filling up as the winter influenza took its toll. Many of the older men couldn't cope with the basic conditions in the camps. They came to Alex with coughs and wheezing that only a spell in the warmth of the hospital with a little caring attention could cure. Alex fretted about them as she discharged them and sent them back to the rigours of camp life, but she knew that for most of them it was the only home they had. They wouldn't thank her for preventing them from returning.

Her health centre was put on hold. It was another two weeks before the hospital board met. Alex fumed privately, but there was nothing she could do about it. Margaret smiled pityingly at her every time they met, and Alex had to restrain an urge to slap her lovely face.

Saturday night was on her before she knew it, and she fought down a rising sense of panic. She had hardly seen Andrew during the week except for behind a mask in theatre, and had almost convinced herself that she was fully in control of her emotions. As the hour approached when Andrew would pick her up she grew doubtful again.

She eyed herself cautiously in the mirror. The figure before her seemed not to belong to her. Her big eyes, dark with fatigue from the busy week, looked seriously at her. She had gone to some trouble with her hair and make-up. Her hair shone with a fiery glow, framing her pale face. The green dress would have done a fashion house proud. She twisted round. The white of the skin on her back make a startling contrast to the deep green of the dress. It was too bare, she thought.

The sound of a loud knock on the door made her jump. Alex glanced at her watch. She couldn't face him. Seven-thirty—the man was disgustingly punctual! Her stomach tightened into a knot and she opened the door.

Andrew was in a deep grey suit, the first time Alex had seen him formally dressed, and she caught her breath at the sheer good looks of the man. He filled her doorway, his blue eyes crinkling in appreciation at the sight of her. For a moment they stood still.

'Aren't you going to ask me in?'

Alex recovered herself and stood aside to let him past.

'I'm sorry. Would you like a drink? A beer?'

He stood in the centre of the room, filling the place with his presence.

'No.'

She looked at him questioningly. He hesitated.

'I'm sorry, that wasn't me at my polite best.' He picked up a magazine from the coffee-table and flicked through it before throwing it back. 'Alex, we'd better get out of here if I'm going to keep my promise to you. You look magnificent!' He walked back to the door and pulled it open. 'Let's go.' He threw the words almost roughly at her.

They drove to the hall in strained silence. Alex strove to think of something impersonal to say, but her attempts at conversation fell sadly flat. Andrew drove with his hands clenched hard on the steering-wheel. He was tired too, Alex thought. It had been a busy week for them both.

The hall was packed with what seemed the entire population of the town. Con and Janet waved furiously from their table, and Andrew fought to make a path through to them.

'Who won?' whispered Alex furiously. In her preparation she had forgotten to find out.

'Brawton.'

'Oh, no!'

To her surprise Con greeted them cheerfully. At the table made up predominantly of Kinley players and their partners there seemed to be no lack of good humour. As Alex commiserated they reassured her.

'It's OK, Doc. We've won three years in a row, it's probably about time we got done. Forget about it and have a good time.'

They were intent on doing just that, it seemed. After a huge smorgasbord meal the tables were pushed back and the dancing began in earnest. During the meal Alex relaxed and enjoyed herself, but as the music began she felt the tension re-surface. Andrew led her on to the dance-floor.

They moved well together. Around them couples were doing an assortment of dancing. Although it was a foxtrot tune many were dancing in the modern style, without touching each other, but Andrew held her firmly. She was a good dancer and their movements were well matched. She was aware of the scores of single men around the walls watching the couples with blatant envy. A single girl's dream!

she thought.

Andrew was not sharing. He was quiet, and they moved from one dance to the next without speaking. Their bodies moulded perfectly to each other—too well, she thought. The tension increased between them to the point where it became unbearable. Andrew's hands, lightly resting on the bare skin of her back, set her nerves alight. She felt as if she were a wire, stretched to breaking-point. Suddenly she could bear it no longer. She excused herself and made her way to the ladies' room.

Janet saw her go and followed her. She stood against the basins and eyed Alex with concern.

'You two aren't exactly a bundle of fun tonight,' she observed.

'I know.' Alex spread her hands helplessly. 'I don't know what to do. It's a disaster!'

Janet was silent for a moment, then said, 'Well, what about sharing yourself around a bit? If you can't have fun with Andrew McIntyre for heaven's sake have fun with someone else!'

Alex shook her head. They returned to the hall, and as they reached the door they were pounced on by two eager loggers. Janet laughed and looked expressively at Alex. In the distance Alex could see Andrew, chatting at the table with Con. As Janet was whirled on to the floor Alex inwardly shrugged her shoulders. She turned back to her prospective partner, who grabbed her with delight and spun her into a dance.

She didn't stop all night. As soon as the loggers realised she was available she was claimed by one after the other, and to her surprise she found she was enjoying herself. The sheer physical energy of keeping up to her partners drove Andrew from her mind. She whirled from one partner to another, struggling to give each her undivided attention. As the evening wore on the dancing slowed down. The effort became too much and she found her attention going back to Andrew.

The dancers started to disperse. The band struck up a slow, lingering number. The man she was with pulled her closer, and Alex stiffened. She was suddenly aware of a hand on her partner's shoulder and Andrew moving across to take his place.

'Having fun?'

His smile was glittering and dangerous. His hands pulled her close and their bodies moved rhythmically together. Alex was tired and felt a sudden absurd desire to weep.

'Come on, little one, I'll take you home.'

The words were gentle, but the voice was hard and expressionless. Alex looked up at him wonderingly and tried to pull away, but he caught her hand and held it in a grip that brooked no opposition. She was led back to their table. They said their farewells mechanically and joined the steady stream of revellers wending their way home.

Andrew handed Alex into the Land Rover and drove the short distance to the hospital. Alex couldn't speak. Her teeth were chattering and she hugged herself to try and stop shivering. She knew the cause wasn't just the cold.

They stopped in the car park, but Andrew didn't leave her to go to his own quarters. He walked beside her to the door of her flat and waited patiently while she fumbled with the key.

'Ask me in, Alex.'

She looked questioningly up at him and he took the key from her fingers and opened the door. He pushed her gently through the door and followed her in.

She had left the heater on, and the flat was a haven of warmth after the chill of the night air. Shaking off the feeling of unreality, she turned to him.

'Would you like a coffee?'

'Thank you.'

She busied herself in the kitchenette, striving to ignore his presence. He stood, his back to the heater, gravely watching her.

They drank their coffee standing on the thick pile rug in front of the gas fire. Andrew never let his eyes leave her face. When she had finished he took her cup from her fingers and put it on the mantelpiece. He placed his hands under her chin, forcing her eyes up to meet him.

'Why are you so afraid, Alex?' he asked softly.

'I'm not afraid.'

'No?'

She tried to drag her eyes away, but his hands held her face towards his.

'Alex, we're so right—you must be able to feel it. Our bodies tonight were perfect for each other, and I had to sit and watch other men hold you. You're not going to do that to me again, Alex, do you hear?'

She shook her head mutely.

'You won't.' He reached down and seized her shoulders. 'You're mine, Alex Donell, and you know you are!'

He pulled her roughly to him, holding her fiercely against him. His hands tightened around her, his face settled in her hair. For a long moment Alex held herself tense. To give in to this man was to betray all she had worked so hard to achieve in the past six years.

'Alex!' His hand came under her chin again and his eyes

were dark with passion. 'You're mine!'

His mouth came down on hers. His hands moved back to hold her hard against him, lifting her up to meet his demanding kiss.

Alex felt her resistance crumble. Her senses swam. This man, this mouth against hers, was the only thing that mattered. Her lips parted gently, welcomingly. She felt her tongue come out and tentatively explore the cavern of his mouth. Her hands came from her sides, softly feeling the roughness of his cheeks. Deep within her a forgotten need awakened and grew. He warmed her, sending every nerve aching to hold him closer.

He pushed her back from him and stood, searching her eyes. His gaze asked a question, probing her heart. His expression sent a surge of joy through her body. This man, this blond giant, loved her. She felt her eyes prick with tears and his fingers came up to trace the course of a teardrop down her cheek.

With infinite gentleness his hands explored her body. They caressed the naked skin of her back and found an entrance there to the quivering delight beyond. The dress did not allow the restriction of a bra. His fingers fondled the firm roundness of her breasts, caressing, fingering, teasing each hard nipple, leaving her aching with pleasure. His hands moved lower, searching for knowledge of her hidden secrets. Every vestige of resistance was gone. Alex's hands moved over him, holding him closer, closer.

With a sigh of exquisite pleasure Andrew pulled away from her. He caught her hands and held them, looking down into her lovely face.

'You'll marry me, my heart?'

She shook her head numbly, instinctively. *Marry*. The

word caught her with a stab of pain. Her eyes shut, trying to block out unwelcome shafts of memory. Andrew placed his fingers on her eyelids, stroking the soft skin with a feather-light touch.

'I said I wouldn't rush you, but I'm a liar, little one. I can't look at you and not have you. You're part of me. I'm claiming my own.'

His arms went round her again, gently rocking her back and forth. Alex tried to pull back, but the arms held her. She couldn't fight him; her body betrayed her. She looked up at him and the eyes crinkled down at her. He laughed, a low, joyful laugh.

'Admit it, Alex Donell.'

His mouth came down again. His arms reached up and slipped the soft wool crêpe from her shoulders, and the dress slipped downward. His hands reached down and folded her body up to his, cradling her to him. Their kiss lasted forever. When it was over they were in the pretty blue bedroom. The soft counterpane was caressing and their bodies were one.

Alex woke as the first flicker of dawn filtered through the curtains. For a moment she lay secure and warm. Andrew's body was curved around her own, his arm flung over her, possessive even in sleep. A deep feeling of peace and utter contentment flowed through her body. She lay for a moment pretending to herself that what he suggested could be. Marriage to Andrew—her body cried out in delight at the prospect. The intimacy of his skin against hers sent tremors of love sweeping over her. Gently she eased herself from under the encircling arm. Andrew stirred in his sleep but didn't wake. His blond head lay peacefully on the pillows, and Alex's heart went out to him. Resolutely she collected

jeans and a sweater and made her way through to the
bathroom.

She showered and dressed and returned to the living-room.
The green dress was still lying in a crumpled heap in front of
the fire. She tidied the place automatically and made herself
a cup of coffee, then sat with it trying to get her mind to think
clearly.

Her thoughts went back, over the time of her marriage. The
pain and the loneliness her dependence on Chris had caused
welled within her. The nights she had ached for him, fretting
until she was convinced some disaster had befallen him,
crowded back into her mind. She thought of Timmy and her
overwhelming love for him. How could she commit herself
to that demanding love again, the love that left her exposed
to such heartache and despair? She fought back the joy of the
night, the longing to be back under Andrew's encircling arm.
She had felt like this before, when one man had been her
world. By the time Andrew emerged sleepily from the
bedroom, knotting his tie as he came out, she was holding a
cold cup, staring bleakly into the flames.

She stared sightlessly up at him. He came towards her, his
look concerned and tender. She stood up and warded him off
with her hands.

'You'd better go.'

Her voice was devoid of any emotion. Her face was still.

'Alex . . .'

'Please—get out.'

He stood looking at her for a long moment. The silence
stretched interminably.

'Alex, don't do this to yourself.' He reached a hand out,
but she stepped back.

'Get out!'

His expression hardened.

'You're mine, Alex. I claim my own.'

'I'm nobody's.' Her voice raised. 'I belong to nobody except to me. I won't depend on you or anybody else! I am not going to be hurt again. Now are you going to get out or am I going to start screaming?'

Her voice broke on a sob, but as he reached towards her she pulled herself up and looked him full in the face. His eyes met hers, anger meeting anger. He reached down to the armchair where his coat had been dropped the night before, flung it over his shoulder and left the flat.

Alex waited until she could no longer hear the footsteps receding down the corridor, then went back into the bedroom. She buried her face in the pillow moulded by his head and burst into racking sobs. What had her freedom cost?

CHAPTER EIGHT

SUNDAY was interminable. Alex made repairs to her ravaged face and did her rounds, mechanically responding to her patients' conversation. Andrew's Land Rover was still in the hospital car park, but where he was she didn't know. She went back to her flat and made herself a cold lunch, then sat before the fire and gazed bleakly into the future. How could she continue working beside Andrew with what lay between them? She knew the situation was intolerable, yet the thought of leaving the valley filled her with panic. For a little while her mind betrayed her into imagining life as Andrew's wife, but always the memory of the aching dependence she had once had and the devastation of the loss that followed it blocked out her love for him.

It was love. She admitted it even to herself, and the knowledge caused a stabbing pain deep within her. He couldn't be allowed to come close to her again. When she was apart from him she could reason, but when they were together she saw nothing but a pair of laughing blue eyes that made her mind and body offer everything they had.

The flat was closing in on her. It felt desolate. Even the cat had deserted her and gone to hunt in the nearby bush. Alex threw on her coat and walking boots and left the building.

Down behind the hospital a walking track meandered along a fast-running creek of icy water, run off from the snow-capped peaks above them. Alex set off, not knowing where the track was going but only knowing that she needed to walk, to get away from the confines of her flat. The track was slippery with clay and several times she caught herself from falling. It was rough going and she found she had to concentrate. The silence apart from the rushing of the water over the stones was balm to her. Once she stopped to allow a prickly little echidna to waddle across the path in front of her. It seemed oblivious of her presence. Entranced, she followed its path until it disappeared into the bushes.

After a couple of hours' hard walking she found her mind was becoming calmer. The muddled jumble of thought settled, leaving her accepting the rightness of her decision. She turned about to retrace her steps, resolute in the decision to stay at the hospital and stick out the difficult adjustment she and Andrew had to make. We're mature adults, she told herself firmly. We can surely behave like that and find a basis on which we can work. Overriding everything was a voice in the back of her head crying, I don't want to leave.

The walk back was uphill and harder. Alex's feet were still tender and she was glad to see the long white building appear through the trees. Dusk was starting to fall. A couple of cheeky wallabies were already out, grazing on the lawns at the rear of the hospital. Their heads came up as she approached and they made a couple of token hops away, but before she was out of sight their heads were back down, munching on the new green shoots of grass.

Alex pushed open the flat door, sighing with weariness. Janet was sitting on the mat, playing, with the big black tom. She looked up as Alex entered, her cheeks pink with excitement.

'Where have you been?' Her voice was accusing. 'We've been waiting for an hour, haven't we, puss?' The cat cast Alex a baleful glance from the comfort of Janet's lap. 'And Tom's hungry.'

Alex laughed.

'Not he! If he hasn't caught a mouse or wheedled something from the kitchen staff I don't know Tom.' She looked closely at Janet, putting aside her distress in the pleasure of seeing her. 'What's happened?'

'What do you mean, what's happened?' Janet's voice was carefully innocent.

'Janet Davis, you're bursting with news! Would you like to tell me or, do I have to sit on you?'

Janet's colour rose. She gave Alex a sheepish grin and held out her left hand. On her third finger lay a beautiful sapphire, surrounded by a cluster of tiny diamonds.

Alex smiled at her friend. The pain of her day eased in the face of Janet's transparent happiness. They hugged, and Alex foraged in the fridge for a bottle of wine.

'It should be champagne, I know,' she apologised, raising her glass, 'but my fridge won't run to it. Next time, give me some warning.'

Janet beamed with delight.

'Isn't it wonderful what finishing the football season can do? All of a sudden they think, what am I going to do with the next six months?'

'Might as well get married, I suppose,' Alex finished for her. 'Janet, it's great news. He's lovely!'

'I know.'

They looked at each other and burst out laughing.

'It seems so unreal,' confessed Janet.

'Wait till you're head cook and bottle-washer for Con and six little Cons,' Alex warned. 'Then it'll seem real enough!'

'There speaks a true romantic,' Janet retorted. She put

down her glass. 'I went to tell Mrs Mac while I waited for you.' Her face clouded a little. 'She's tickled pink, but I think it hurts that she won't make the wedding. It seems to me that she's picked up in the last few days, but there's no way she could cope with a wedding, is there?'

Alex shook her head, and Janet grimaced.

'Well, I guess I can't have everything. Con's round with Andrew. Shall we go and join them?'

'No!' Alex's voice was sharp. 'Sorry, Janet, but I'd rather not. I'll see Con soon enough and you can give him a kiss of congratulations for me.'

Janet was looking closely at Alex.

'Alex dear, what's wrong?' she asked anxiously.

'Nothing a little separation from Andrew McIntyre won't cure.' The words sounded forced even to Alex, but she dredged up a smile and pushed Janet to the door. 'Go on and join your beloved. It's lovely news.'

Janet's answering smile was troubled. She stopped at the door and looked back.

'I so hoped it would be good for you last night. I'm sorry.' She hesitated, then continued, 'Alex, my mum's putting on an engagement celebration on Thursday night. I know Con wants Andrew and I'd really like you to be there. Do you think you can bear it? It won't be just you and him. If I know my mum half the valley will be there!'

'Don't be daft!' Alex smiled reassuringly. 'Wild horses couldn't drag me away!'

The thought filled her with dismay. Janet eyed her doubtfully, but her wish for Alex to attend overcame her suspicion that Alex was being less than truthful. With a wave of her jewelled hand she departed, back to a true celebration with Andrew and Con. Alex was left with an aching longing to be with them.

She made a token attempt at preparing an evening meal, then climbed into bed and lay looking at the slivers of moonlight making patterns on the ceiling. Her eyes stayed wide and sleepless. The phone's shrill ring made her jump.

'Alex?'

'I don't want to talk to you.'

'Alex——'

'No!'

She slammed the phone down and went back to her concentration on the ceiling.

CHAPTER NINE

THE short spell of dry weather broke on Monday and Alex woke up to torrential rain and gale-force winds. No matter how well covered she was it was impossible to get from the car park into the hospital without being soaked. Margaret fought a losing battle to keep the mud out of the corridors, but it involved doing a complete clean after each outpatient or visitor entered the building. The drive up to Brawton was a nightmare. Visibility was down to less than ten feet and the edges of the road were treacherous. Alex added half an hour to her normal travelling time and still arrived late.

Two road accidents in the week meant that she and Andrew were thrown together as they did their best to repair the damage to the victims. Luckily for them both, and for the patients too, Alex reflected, they could both ignore personal problems when they were working. As they operated side by side they might just have well have been chance colleagues. As soon as the surgery was finished Alex bolted, ignoring the construction the theatre staff were likely to place on her behaviour. Neither of the crashes were very serious, but it had the effect of slowing Alex's driving down still further.

Alex was tense and tired, and as the week went by her fatigue increased.She told herself it was the work, but knew it was only part of the reason. Surreptitious glances at Andrew showed that he was looking as strained as she was, and guilt added to her anxiety.

She worked in a kind of limbo. One part of her was functioning on a normal level. She saw her patients and listened with attention to their problems. She joked with the men and found enjoyment in the easy rapport that had grown between them. Janet bounced around the wards in high good humour. She had obviously decided Alex needed cheering up, and went out of her way to do just that. On Tuesday afternoon out at Brawton Alex unpacked her dressings to apply a cover to an injection site. All her small sticking plasters had been replaced with the stock from the children's ward. Her burly patient left wearing a bemused expression and a sticking plaster covered in pictures of Winnie the Pooh and Tigger. Alex found she could still laugh, but the thought of Andrew was never far from her mind.

Mrs Mac added to her feeling of unreality. She was dying inexorably, and her courage made Alex want to weep. She refused to complain. When pressed she admitted to a little itchiness and conceded that she felt too nauseated to eat, but they were the only symptoms she would admit to. Alex knew there was pain, she could see it in her eyes, but she wouldn't admit to it.

Alex swallowed her pride and asked Andrew to give his opinion. It hurt to have to do it, but she wouldn't let Mrs Mac suffer because of her own stupid emotional problems. Andrew examined her, but there was little he could find to alter. Stemetil for the nausea and morphine for the pain the lady refused to concede she had—there was little else.

When they were in the room together Mrs Mac looked anxiously from one to the other. As Andrew left she turned to Alex.

'What's wrong, dear?' she asked.

'What do you mean?' Alex tried for a bright note, but it didn't quite come off.

Mrs Mac looked at her for a long moment.

'Don't let him slip through your fingers, Alex. I know a
good man when I see one. If I was forty years younger and
not stuck in this hospital bed I'd be out there trying for him
myself!'

Alex shook her head. She could think of nothing to say.

Andrew stopped her in the hospital corridor on Wednesday
night.

'Are you going to Con's and Janet's party tomorrow
night?' The question was terse and his expression was grim.

'Yes.' Her voice was a whisper.

'I'll pick you up at eight.'

'No.' Her voice fell away, then suddenly found itself. 'I'll
make my own way there, thank you.'

'As you wish.' The words were rough and hurtful. He
turned and left her looking helplessly after him.

Alex arrived early at Janet's party. She had agonised over
what to wear, rightly deeming the green dress inappropriate.
She had finally decided on a flowing wool skirt in soft grey
and a high-throated white shirt with big flounces. She pulled
her hair up and fastened it with silver combs. Her normally
pale complexion was almost translucent with her lack of
sleep. Ruthlessly she applied blusher, but the dark shadows
seemed to deepen.

Con and Janet were waiting to receive their guests, and
Alex put aside her own unhappiness in the face of their joy.
She gave Con a kiss and he hugged her warmly. She had
known Janet and Con for such a short time, yet already they
were friends she valued. It was a big, noisy, happy party. The
house swelled as the entire staff of the bank, the full nursing
staff and anyone in the valley who considered themselves a
friend wedged their way in. The kitchen was set aside for
refreshments, and the table groaned with a typical country

supper, sausage rolls and sandwiches, asparagus rolls, cream sponges, ginger fluffs, pavlovas and cheesecakes and trays of mouth-watering lamingtons. Big urns dispensed tea and coffee and wine casks were set up on the sideboard, but most of the men found refreshment more to their taste from a keg on the back veranda.

The big lounge-room was reserved for dancing. An elderly patient of Alex's thumped away at the piano, while her husband stood beside her, fiddling furiously. Their music wouldn't win any prizes, but it was foot-tapping stuff. Already a few couples were energetically twirling around the room.

Alex settled down in the kitchen. Con's mother buttonholed her and Alex tried to concentrate on what she was saying, but her attention kept swinging back to the door, watching the late arrivals. The party was well under way when Andrew and Margaret walked in. They entered laughing with Margaret clinging to Andrew's arm. His gaze was on her face and his hand held hers proprietorially.

She was gorgeous. She wore a dress of rich crimson silk, tightly cut to reveal every detail of her exquisite figure. Her blonde hair was piled elegantly into a mass of golden curls, and tiny diamonds flashed in her ears. Her laughing face left Andrew's momentarily to congratulate Con and Janet before searching out and again holding Andrew's attention to herself. She cast every other woman in the room into the shade.

Janet's agonised gaze found Alex, but Alex had herself under control. What right had she to feel this pain? She had rejected Andrew, so it was only natural he should turn to someone else. She turned back to Con's mother to find her eyeing Margaret disparagingly.

'I don't know what she's trying to prove, coming to a party like this in that get-up.' She sniffed. 'I'm surprised she came at all. Janet only asked her because she felt she had to—she's always made it obvious that Janet was beneath her touch. As we all are. Well, I'm not one to criticise. Each to his own, I say,' she went on obscurely. 'Will you excuse me, my dear? I think Janet's mum might need some help.' She moved ponderously off, obviously itching to discuss the new arrivals with someone a little more receptive than Alex.

Alex was left staring at the supper table. The sight of so much food made her feel ill. She made her way to the door. The dancing in the other room had livened up and the room was crowded with moving bodies. Once inside she was seized; in this town there was never any danger of becoming a wallflower. She was passed from one partner to another, and if her attention seemed to wander or her answers seemed mechanical no one seemed to notice. After a while Andrew and Margaret took the floor. He held her close, in fact the tiny area available for dancing left him little choice, but that didn't alleviate Alex's misery. A couple of times they brushed Alex as they passed and Alex had to fight to stop herself from shuddering. Finally she could bear it no longer. She went to find Janet. As she approached her Janet's angry eyes met hers.

'The creep!' Janet exploded indignantly. 'Fancy doing this to you, and at my party too!'

'Janet,' Alex's voice was soft, 'I haven't got any claim on him, you know.'

'Well!' Janet sounded cross. 'If you'd played your cards right you could have, I'm sure, instead of leaving him to that . . . to that . . .' Words failed her.

Alex shook her head

Con approached and effectively stopped all conversation

by giving Alex a huge bear-hug.

'Going already?' he queried.

'I'm dead beat, Con. Forgive me, but I must.' Alex held him at arm's length and laughed up at him. 'It's a lovely party, but I'm not as young as you two, you know.'

'There spake the greybeard,' Janet agreed. 'Off you go, you poor old dear. Shall I ring the night staff and ask them to pop in and help you into bed?'

Alex laughed and retreated, leaving them looking after her with concern. She had the feeling they saw a lot more than she would like them to guess.

There was more for the town to gossip over in the next few days than the love life of the medical staff. The rain fell relentlessly. On Saturday Alex squelched down to the creek behind the hospital and found it a foaming, raging river bursting its banks on either side and hurling masses of debris in its path. There were flood warnings out for all the rivers, but for the first time, as Alex stood and watched the surging body of water, she felt disquiet. She squelched back to the main building and entered the office.

Margarét was there, sitting at her desk. She looked pointedly at the puddle of water dripping from Alex's coat. Alex looked down and grinned ruefully.

'Sorry, Maggie.'

The woman flinched. Whoops, thought Alex, I've done it again! She bit her lip, then caught herself. This formality with names was ridiculous.

'I've just been down to the creek,' she went on determinedly. 'I can't believe how much it's risen. Shouldn't we be filling sandbags or something?'

She was given a faint, supercilious smile. 'I don't think we have any reason to worry, Dr Donell.'

Margaret bent her head back over her work, and Alex gritted her teeth. Why did this woman persist in trying to make her feel like a six-year-old? She turned to leave and collided with Andrew coming in. He caught her arms and steadied her, and she flushed and drew back. She was aware of Margaret looking up. Margaret's smile had deepened and a faint blush came over her face. Andrew looked from one to the other, and Alex was uneasily aware of her dripping waterproofs compared to Margaret's trim uniform.

'Is there a problem?' Andrew's voice was brusque.

'Dr Donell is worried that we're all going to be swept away in the floods.' Margaret's voice was sweetly humorous. Andrew laughed and Alex stalked out of the room. They could have each other!

'Alex!'

Andrew followed her. She heard his brief exchange with Margaret and footsteps striding down the corridor after her. Suppressing a desire to escape at a run, she turned to face him.

'Yes?' Her voice was tight.

'I'm sorry, that was rude of us. In fact, we're in for trouble, but hopefully not with the creek. We must be a good thirty feet above the level of the creek, and if we were flooded the whole valley would be under water.'

'I see.' Alex stood feeling slightly silly. She waited for him to continue, achingly aware of the tension and lines of fatigue on the face in front of her.

'There's been a mudslide on the road between here and Brawton,' Andrew told her. 'The road's impassable. There are men out trying to clear the mess, but with this rain continuing the whole hillside is unstable. I don't think they're going to be able to clear it for a while.'

'Does that mean I'm going to be able to sleep in on Monday morning, then?' she asked, attempting to smile.

He smiled back.

'I guess so. We can only hope that we're not needed out there. Normally we can get the company helicopter, but with these conditions I think every 'copter in the state is going to be in use.'

'We'll cross our fingers, then.'

'We'll do that.' His tone was serious.

Alex looked up into his eyes. The urge to smooth away the lines of worry was almost irresistible. She winced and looked away.

'Is that all?' she asked.

'No.'

Her glance went up involuntarily to his face. His expression was grim.

'We need to talk.'

'No!' Alex backed away and went to turn. His hand reached out and caught her, holding her fast.

'It's not my habit to sleep with someone and never talk to them again, no matter what you may be used to.'

Alex gasped. Before she could help herself her hand reached up and gave him a ringing slap across his cheek. He caught it and held it, looking sardonically down into her eyes.

'Well, well, well—anger! The cool Alex Donell is capable of showing some emotion after all!'

'Let me go!' Her voice was a furious whisper. She pulled her arm back, but Andrew's grip tightened. She cast a frantic glance down the hospital corridor, but the place was deserted. He pushed her face up, forcing her to look at him.

'You can't do this, Alex,' he muttered. 'You're driving me

crazy!'

'Oh? I thought you were getting over me amazingly well. You and Maggie can begin again exactly where you left off.'

'What does that mean?' His tone was dangerous.

'I wouldn't have a clue,' she replied truthfully. 'And I don't care. Just let me be.'

'What the hell's eating you?' he demanded angrily.

'Nothing.' Her voice lowered and became ice-calm. 'I just don't want to get involved.'

'I've got news for you, lady.' Andrew tightened his grip and pulled her closer. 'You already are involved. You're not an ice maiden, no matter how hard you try to kid yourself that you are. You can't pretend about what happened to us the other night. You want me just as much as I want you, don't you, Dr Alex Donell?'

'No!' Her voice broke on a sob.

He gazed down at her, his anger tangible in the air between them. Alex stood passive, waiting for him to let her go. Baffled fury centred on her. With any other man she would have been frightened. As it was she waited, limp in his hold. She knew she had nothing to fear.

His voice, when it finally came, was tired and defeated.

'Go on, then, Alex. Do what you have to do.'

His hand pushed her away and she stood watching as he retreated down the corridor. She felt desolate and very much alone. Her fingers hurt where his grip had held her and she rubbed them absently. She was suddenly aware of the office reception window, wide open at the end of the hall. Margaret would have heard everything they said. She shook her head in a gesture of confusion and retreated to her flat.

She changed and went to sit for a while with Mrs Mac. In this room at least she felt at peace. For the last couple of days

Mrs Mac had been drifting in and out of consciousness, only dimly aware that Alex was in the room. Alex thought it was as much for herself as for Mrs Mac that she continued to spend all the time she could spare with her.

She spent the rest of the day wading through a mound of paperwork. She worked steadily, using the repetitive work to take her mind off anything else. The big tomcat lay at her feet, and she found his presence strangely comforting. Her hand would creep down and rub his ears as he slept. Independant career woman, she thought. What a joke!

Just after shift change that night Margaret came to the apartment. Alex had washed her hair and was sitting in front of the heater towelling it dry. She was wearing her big towelling bathrobe and slippers and looked ruefully down at herself before answering the door. Anyone who came visiting this late at night deserved everything they got! She swung open the door to Margaret.

'Can I come in?'

'Please.' Alex stood back and allowed Margaret to enter.

The woman walked over to the mat and stood with her back to the heater waiting for Alex to shut the door and follow her. Alex was left feeling like a naughty schoolgirl in the headmistress's office.

'What can I do for you, Margaret?' she asked.

'You can leave.'

Alex's eyes flew to Margaret's face. The girl was watching her with hard eyes.

'I beg your pardon?'

'You heard me,' said Margaret icily.

'I think you're going to have to explain.' Alex looked at her with a rising sense of disbelief.

'It's simple. You're going to have to pack your bags and

get out of this valley, Dr Alex Donell. You're not wanted.'

Alex gaped at the girl in stupefaction.

'What on earth are you talking about?'

'I'm talking about Dr McIntyre. Andrew.'

'Well?' I can't believe this is happening, Alex thought. The other girl was watching her, her eyes filled with venom.

'You know damn well that he thinks he's in love with you!'

'And if he is?'

'He's not!' Margaret spat the words at her. 'He's so tired he's ready to imagine anything. Don't you understand? He's at the point of absolute exhaustion, and you can't see past your pretty little face that you're driving him into the ground!'

'No,' said Alex. 'You're right—I don't see.'

'The work in this valley is too much for two doctors, let alone one,' Margaret went on. 'We need someone who can pull their weight. Andrew is on the point of collapse, and what does he get? A woman. You!'

Alex shook her head, letting the words flow over her. There was no way she could defend herself.

Margaret spread her hands in front of her and stood regarding the perfectly manicured nails. Her voice continued, beautifully modulated, each word weighed and considered.

'You're a doctor, you know what exhaustion can do to a man. Andrew is past the point of reason. He was holding out waiting for an assistant, and now he has you. He can't think straight any more. He's giving you a few easy little jobs and is still bearing the brunt himself, and now he's imagining himself emotionally entangled with you.'

Alex gasped. 'That's not true! I'm carrying my share of the load.'

'Are you?' The smooth voice was laced with hate. 'Do you

know how hard he's working? Have you bothered to find out?'

Alex flushed. It was true she had carried out the work Andrew gave her without enquiring further, but she had imagined it to be a fair proportion of the workload.

'Of course you haven't. You don't give a damn about the man, do you?'

Silence. The two faced each other. Alex's towel had slipped from around her hair and was hanging damply about her shoulders. She pulled it free and absently rubbed at the damp curls, waiting for what was coming.

Margaret shrugged. Once again she scrutinised her nails.

'Well, I do—I don't mind admitting it. Andrew and I have known each other since he was in medical school. He came to see me when he got this job and begged me to join him. We make a great partnership, and I'm not going to let some snip of a trainee doctor interfere with it.'

'You might not have a choice.' Alex was white with anger, her voice was trembling.

The other girl shook her head. Her eyes came up, cold and calculating, and looked at her.

'You've got a conscience. You know damn well that you're destroying him. Get out of this valley and let someone else come in, someone who can work with Andrew and take the load off his shoulders.'

'And if I don't?' asked Alex calmly.

'You haven't got a choice. You can either go voluntarily or Andrew will finally have to sack you. He'll come to his senses in time. Goodnight, Dr Donell.'

Margaret gave Alex one last contemptuous look before walking to the door.

Alex stood staring at the open door. In a daze she walked

over and shut it, then stood with her back to it as if to stop any other unwelcome intruder. She was shaking uncontrollably, either from shock or anger or a mixture of both. With an effort she willed herself to be calm, to think dispassionately over what Margaret had said.

It was true that Andrew looked tired. He had looked exhausted on the first day she arrived, and the look had not disappeared. How much of the workload had he handed over? There was only one way to find out, and that was to approach him directly. She could do a lot more.

Would he let her, though? And would his tension ease if he did allow her to take over more of his load? The image of his drawn face came to her, and she accepted the fact that he loved her. Or thought he loved her, she corrected herself, remembering Margaret's summing up of the situation. Perhaps Margaret was right and his emotions were being swayed by his fatigue.

Her heart contracted in pain. Her independence, so desperately sought, was costing them both dearly. If this pain was going to stay with her and if it was going to weigh Andrew down was she right to stay?

She sat down again in front of the fire and started pulling a comb through her tangled curls. She tugged roughly, finding solace in inflicting pain on herself. She realised she was crying, steady silent tears coursing down her cheeks. She wiped them away angrily.

To leave this valley was to give in, to run away, she told herself. A tiny voice whispered, 'If you go away you could never see him again.'

Good, she told herself. He's an overbearing, opinionated male who thinks he can sweep you off your feet.

'And don't you want to be swept off your feet?' the little

voice prodded.

'No, I don't,' she said out loud, and jumped at the breaking of the flat's silence.

'Well, what do you want?' the little voice probed.

'I want my mother!' wailed Dr Alex Donell.

She had just climbed into bed when someone scratched at her bedroom door. Uttering a swear word under her breath, Alex donned her robe and went to answer it. The night charge sister stood there, a worried look on her face.

'I'm sorry to bother you, Dr Donell, but we've got a little boy in Children's who's pulled out his drip. We've been trying to contact Dr McIntyre, but he's out on another call and isn't answering our radio messages.'

Alex was perturbed.

'Sure,' she responded. 'I'll just pull some clothes on. You could have contacted me first, you know. Is it Sammy Neil?'

'Yes.'

'Well, he is my patient. I'd expect you to call me.'

'Dr McIntyre usually does the night work himself,' Sister explained.

Alex grinned at the girl. 'The man's a workaholic! If they're my patients, I look after them, OK?'

The sister's worried look faded and she smiled back.

'And from here on in I'll take my share of night calls.'

Alex left the night sister to return to the ward while she slipped on a skirt and jumper and followed her.

Sammy was wide awake and interested. It took Alex a few minutes to reinsert the drip into his the back of his chubby little hand. As he settled she stayed chatting to the sister in the darkened ward. While they were talking they heard Andrew's Land Rover pull into the hospital car park. At least he can go straight to bed now, thought Alex. They finished talking and Alex made her way down the corridor to her flat. As she passed Andrew's office she noted a crack of light under the door, and on impulse she knocked.

'Come in.'

Andrew was sitting at his desk, a huge pile of papers in front of him. He looked up as she came in and the worry lines deepened.

'What on earth are you doing?' she demanded.

'What does it look like?'

Alex picked up the top couple of papers and recognised the same type of paperwork she had been doing that afternoon in front of the fire—legal letters, medical compensation forms, referral letters and other odds and ends of medical correspondence. The difference was in the size of the piles. Andrew's was nearly a foot high.

'This is crazy!' she exclaimed. 'You should be in bed!'

'I know.' He smiled wearily. 'These have got to be done at some stage, though.'

'How come you're so far behind?'

He sighed and put down his pen.

'For two months before you came we didn't have another doctor. Anything that could be put off was put off. Now I'm paying the price.'

Alex looked at the pile.

'Can I help?' she asked.

'I don't see how you can. All this stuff relates to patients I've seen. It's me that's got to do it.'

He picked up his pen again and ran his hand through his hair. Alex's heart did a sudden lurch.

'Look, you have to go to bed—you're asleep on your feet. You've got clinic at Kinley tomorrow and I can't go to

Brawton. I'll take over at Kinley and you get this lot out of the way.'

The tired blue eyes looked at her steadily.

'The road up there is terrible. I don't want you driving on it.'

'That's ridiculous and you know it,' she retorted. 'I'm as capable of driving in these conditions as you are.'

'There's snow over the road.'

'So what?' Her voice sounded defiant and she grinned inwardly. She even sounded brave! Out loud she said, 'Do I have to fit chains?'

'Yes. We've got them here.' Andrew's voice sounded doubtful.

'Well, that's settled. I'll see you in the morning before I go. Now, Dr McIntyre,' she leaned over the desk and flicked the switch on the desk lamp, 'bed!'

'Really?' He gave her a hopeful look and she managed a laugh.

'Goodnight.'

Alex fled.

CHAPTER TEN

THE next morning was freezing. Alex woke with her nose tingling with the cold. She lay cocooned in her warm quilt, trying to summon up the drive to get out of bed, then reached her hand out to the curtain and flicked it back. The world was glistening white; frost coated everything. The cat was sitting on her bedroom windowsill looking pathetic. She pulled the window back and he joyfully leapt on to the warm little oasis of her bed. Alex winced as the icy air came in with him and dived back under the covers. The cat moved protestingly and resettled on the quilt over her stomach. A knock echoed through the flat.

'Go away!' Alex's voice was muffled through the bedclothes.

She stayed under as footsteps approached the bed, then stuck a cautious nose out to investigate.

'Good morning.'

Janet swooped on the cat and plopped it on the floor, then settled on the end of the bed herself. The cat gave her a look of dislike and moved into the lounge-room.

'What's good about it?' Alex muttered crossly. 'Be an angel, Janet, and turn the heater on.'

'Not worth it,' Janet replied cheerfully. 'You haven't got time for sitting in front of fires this morning. Cook is doing us both a big cooked breakfast in the kitchen. She reckons we'll need it. It's as much as I can do to stop her packing provisions for us for a week.'

'For us?' queried Alex.

'Us.' Janet's response was gleeful. 'Andrew says you're going up to Kinley and you're not to go alone. I'm it. Maggie is not pleased,' she added.

'I don't suppose she would be. Janet, I can cope alone.'

'He said you'd say that. His Lordship's instructions are that you take me or you don't go. Come on, Alex, get up! It could be fun.'

Alex eyed Janet's crisp white uniform doubtfully.

'I know, I know,' Janet went on. 'Look, get up and have breakfast and I'll go home and get changed while you do a ward round. But you've got to get out of that bed.'

With a twitch she had the bedclothes off, leaving a laughing, expostulating Alex cringing on the bare bed. With a swipe at Janet with the pillow she ran for the shower.

They found Andrew in the car park putting chains in the back of Alex's Land Rover. He straightened as the girls approached, his breath making clouds in the still, cold air. His eyes searched Alex's face, his expression concerned. 'Are you sure you can cope?' he asked them. 'The road is going to be treacherous.'

Janet answered for them. She put her hands in her trouser pockets and jutted her jaw aggressively.

'Ain't nuthin' we mountain wimin cain't cope with, Doc. What's a bit of ice and snow? I don't know why you're botherin' with them dang fool chains. Ifen it gets a bit slippery Alex'n me 'll jest push.'

They all laughed, and the two girls climbed in. Andrew stood watching them roar out of the car park, his eyes still perturbed.

Alex hadn't been to Kinley and was interested in the changing scenery. The camp lay in the next valley and the road wound up and over the ranges. The Land Rover putted along slowly, mindful of the slippery roads. When they reached the snow line they stopped and attached the chains. Janet was deft at putting them on, and Alex felt real gratitude for her company. There hadn't been much call for snow chains in Brisbane's tropical climate.

The trees above the snow line were stunted and sparse. Alex found herself admiring the bleakness of the terrain. For today at least the rain had stopped and the sun was sending weak rays down on the scene, turning the whole countryside shimmering white. A plough had been through recently, cutting a giant white gash through the snow. Alex slowed to a crawl, but the Land Rover held to the road steadily and didn't miss a beat. She found she was relaxing, enjoying Janet's company and the freedom of being away from the hospital.

When they finally came down out of the snow and found Kinley, a conglomeration of huts in the same style as Brawton, the manager came out to greet them. He had obviously been on the look-out for them, and Alex wondered whether Andrew had been on the phone with instructions.

They started clinic, and Alex realised how much help Janet could be. She ushered the men in with wounds already cleaned and initial paperwork done. She anticipated Alex's needs. Dressings were prepared and syringes filled. Always there was someone to assist, to hold things in place and to replace equipment. The two of them sped through the work in half the time Alex usually took, enjoying themselves as they did it. Alex thought longingly of a permanent arrangement of a sister accompanying each clinic, but knew she was pipe-dreaming. If she couldn't get Janet for one morning a week for a health centre, she couldn't get a permanent sister for clinics.

By early afternoon they were finished. The men gave them a big lunch and waved them off. The return journey held no real terrors for them, and Alex felt relaxed and happy.

The sun was full out now, turning the snow into a magic carpet of whiteness. As they neared the peak the ground flattened out. Instead of the huge, sweeping slopes the ground dipped and rose in a series of minor runs. Alex pulled over the Jeep and looked at Janet, mischief in her eyes.

'I can't resist this. I've got a couple of plastic bags in the back. Let's go!'

With a whoop of delight Janet leapt out of the car. They staggered up the slope with their bags and sat down, pushing themselves until the slope took over and the ground rushed past them in a long white blur. Breathless with laughter, they lay at the bottom of the slope, then staggered to their feet and tackled the slope again.

An hour later they were soaked to the skin and exhausted. They climbed back into the Land Rover and looked guiltily at each other. Their cheeks were flushed and their hair was clinging damply to their foreheads. Janet giggled.

'All in a day's work, Dr Donell?'

'Occupational therapy, Sister Davis.'

Alex turned the key and the engine roared.

'When are you going to get something done about this noise?' yelled Janet, with her hands to her ears.

'I like it!' Alex yelled back defensively. What she didn't add was that she enjoyed the contrast between her vehicle and a certain little white Porsche. She swung out and began to drive down the mountain. She felt relaxed and happy, ready to face whatever confrontations were in store for her.

The first one happened sooner than she expected. As the snow line receded in the rear-vision mirror, another Land

Rover appeared, coming at a fast rate towards them. As they approached it, it veered off and pulled to the side of the road. With surprise, Alex recognised Andrew's vehicle. She pulled to a halt and climbed out as he approached them. One look at him was enough to tell her he was in no good humour. His face was dark with anger.

'Where the hell have you been?' he demanded.

'Kinley,' she replied helpfully, and waited for the explosion. It came.

'I had the manager at Kinley ring me the moment you left. That was an hour and a half ago. What have you been doing for an hour and a half?'

Behind her Alex heard Janet climbing out of the car. Andrew looked from one to another, taking in their sodden clothes and wet hair.

'Can't you guess?' Alex was determined not to be intimidated. 'I couldn't resist the snow and ordered Janet out for a bit of rest and recreation. I've been supervising,' she added virtuously, and from behind she heard Janet choke.

Andrew gazed at them wordlessly, his face contused with anger. When he found his voice it washed over them in icy waves.

'This is a work day, in case you hadn't realised, Sister Davis. You're needed down at the hospital. As for you, Dr Donell, this country is known for its freak storms. You get through the snow country as fast as you can and don't stop to play silly games, especially when no one knows where you are.' He turned on Janet. 'You should know that.'

Janet turned and looked at the sky. It was a magic day with not a cloud. She turned back to Andrew and spread her hands helplessly. He had turned back to Alex.

'I accepted your offer of help in good faith. If I'd known

it was going to entail half a day of driving around the mountains looking for you I would have been better to have done the clinic myself,' he snapped.

He wheeled back to the other side of the road and slammed the door as he climbed into the Land Rover. The vehicle spun round on the narrow road and disappeared down the mountain.

'Wow!' Janet looked at Alex expressively.

Alex said nothing. She climbed back into the driver's seat and started the engine. She drove with concentration, trying to control the surge of anger and humiliation within her. Janet eyed her with a worried frown, but respected her need for silence. Alex dropped her off outside her parents' house.

'I'll get changed and get Mum to drive me up,' Janet said. 'Don't wait for me.'

Alex drove into the hospital car park to find Andrew's Land Rover already parked and him standing beside it. He waited for her to pull up and approached her window.

'It's the hospital board meeting tonight. If you'd like to present your pet project,' the voice was cold and expressionless, 'you'd better do it tonight. Eight o'clock.' He strode away.

Meaning if I don't do it tonight I'm not going to get another chance, thought Alex miserably. She collected her gear and disappeared to change from her sodden clothing.

Alex prepared dispiritedly for the meeting that night. Her latest encounter with Andrew had burst her brief bubble of fun, leaving her flat and listless. As she brushed her hair, giving it bounce and shine after its afternoon soaking, Margaret's cutting comments resounded in her head. For the first time she admitted to herself that Margaret might be right:

Andrew in his present mood was impossible to work with.

She applied her make-up, dabbing blusher angrily on her pale cheeks. The image of his face, furious in his relief, persisted in her mind. She swore to herself. Who the hell did he think he was, treating her like a stupid child? She didn't want his concern, his dominance, his care. She jammed a couple of side-combs in her hair, glared at herself in the mirror and slammed out of the flat.

The boardroom was already full as Alex entered. Andrew was seated at the end of a large mahogany table. His head was bent over a report and he failed to look up as she came in. Margaret was seated on his right and raised her eyes in cool appraisal as Alex hesitated at the door. The remaining seats were taken by six board members, six solid citizens of Pirrengurra, male, middle-aged and oozing respectability. They were curious too, thought Alex, as she faltered before their concerted gaze. She glared at Margaret, who smiled politely at her and said nothing. Andrew finished the page he was perusing and looked up. With a gesture of irritation he motioned her towards an empty chair.

'Sit down, Alex. We've been waiting for you.' He briefly introduced the board members, and with a sinking heart Alex realised she was facing a board of townspeople rather than representatives of the logging community.

'Is there no one on the board representing the logging companies?' she asked curiously.

'Of course there is.' Andrew's reply was brusque. 'We wouldn't expect them to come down in this weather, though, and the representative from Brawton couldn't make it through the mudslide if he wanted to. Now, let's get started.'

The normal business was dispatched efficiently, and Alex realised she wouldn't have very long to wait before presenting her case. She listened with interest to the operation of the hospital board. Although there was a chairman it seemed to be Andrew who was very much in charge. He moved swiftly from item to item, quietly suggesting, agreeing and moving his ideas across so subtly that in many cases individual board members were left thinking they had made the suggestion themselves. A niggle of doubt crept into Alex's mind. Perhaps it would have been better if she had asked Andrew to present the case for the health centre. Impatiently she pushed the thought aside. She was a big girl now. She schooled herself to sit calmly, waiting for Andrew to ask her to speak. At last he did so.

'We have a request before us from Dr Donell.' He paused and for the first time that night allowed himself to smile at Alex. His eyes warmed her and she took courage from his reassurance. 'I think I should let her outline her ideas herself.'

As he spoke a timid knock sounded on the boardroom door, then the night sister's face appeared and looked around for Andrew.

'I'm sorry to intrude, Dr McIntyre, but Mrs Harris is about to deliver. Could you come?'

'I'll be right there.' Andrew rose and gathered the papers before him. 'Sorry, Alex, but you don't need me. Continue.'

He departed, leaving Alex with a cold feeling of dismay. She gazed despairingly at the closing door, then turned back to six interested faces and one hostile one.

They were polite. Alex outlined her case, dwelling on the loneliness she saw among the young wives of the loggers and the need for a social meeting place, but she could feel their lack of interest in a problem they felt did not concern them. Her confidence crumbled in the face of their indifference and she could hear herself faltering. As her voice trailed off the chairman sat back in his armchair and eyed her speculatively.

'This sounds all very well, Dr Donell, but am I right in my surmise that the health needs of these women are being met by the services already provided by this hospital?'

'Yes,' Alex had to agree. 'However, this is not a meeting place. The women come here on an appointment basis, have their baby checked and go home again. A proper health centre would do much more than just provide for the baby's health.'

'But then,' the chairman's voice was smooth, 'our concern is surely only the health of the mothers and children. I don't see that this is anything we should become involved with.' He looked around the table, finding agreement in the faces before him.

'It needs you, though, to agree to staff the centre. If we don't have a trained sister it can't operate.'

The chairman turned to Margaret.

'Matron, perhaps we're being unfair. You've been in the valley for four years now. What are your views? Do the young women in the valley need this centre?'

Alex dug her nails into her palms and gritted her teeth in anger. She fought to control her rising temper as Margaret destroyed any hope she might have had of getting approval.

'Of course I understand that Dr Donell is very enthusiastic, and her enthusiasm is to be commended. However, often it's easy for a newly trained doctor,' her voice dwelled on the 'newly trained', 'to get carried away on a pet project without fully investigating the facts. I believe I know the valley women well, and I haven't heard of any desire for such a centre.'

'They can't want what they don't know about,' Alex snapped.

'Of course,' Margaret agreed placatingly. 'But what do you think, gentlemen? Would your wives have needed such a centre, or were they capable of meeting people and making their own friends?'

'That's unfair and you know it!' Alex retorted.

'Perhaps.' Margaret smiled sweetly at the men around the table. 'However, even if we were to agree, I just don't know where we would get the staff.' She spread her hands helplessly. 'Dr Donell seems to think trained staff grow on trees.' She smiled her loveliest smile, the board members smiled back and the health centre was rejected. They were polite, apologetic and immovable.

Alex sat at the glossy wooden table as the members filed out, heading for supper before the cold drive home. They addressed jocular remarks to her and Alex responded woodenly but politely.

'She's a little upset,' she heard Margaret addressing them as they retreated down the hall. 'Our Dr Donell does seem to get worked up over trifles.'

Alex slammed her fist down on the table, making the glass of water in front of her jump and splash. Damn them for their insensitivity! Damn Margaret, and damn Dr McIntyre too. They could have their precious hospital! Tears of frustration and anger welled in her eyes. She gathered the notes in front of her, hours of carefully prepared argument shot down by Margaret's saccharine tongue. As she stood up she closed her eyes and accepted the inevitability of the pressures on her. This place was not for her. Andrew McIntyre could have his beloved hospital and his precious Margaret. They deserve each other, she said to herself savagely. She left the boardroom, suppressing with difficulty the urge to slam the door as hard as she could.

Mrs Mac's room was lit and as Alex approached the night sister came out.

'Oh, Dr Donell—I was just coming to find you.' She gestured into the room. 'I don't think the end is far away.'

Alex bit her lip. She nodded to the sister. 'OK, I'll stay with her now.'

She sat by the bed. Her hand reached out and took one of Mrs Mac's in hers. The rasping, uneven breathing filled the room and Alex watched as her chest slowly rose and fell. She waited, finding a calmness in herself. This lady was a friend.

After a while Mrs Mac seemed to rouse. Her eyes opened, moved and found Alex.

'I'm dying, aren't I, dear?'

Alex nodded, her hand still gripping Mrs Mac's.

'You'll stay?'

'Yes.'

The fingers moved weakly in Alex's.

'You and Andrew.' She was fighting to find strength. 'You'll be fine, I know it. All it takes is courage.' She gave a ghost of a smile and her eyes closed again. The rasping breathing continued.

Alex stayed where she was. The night sister passed the door occasionally but did not intrude. They might have had the hospital to themselves.

In the early hours of the morning Alex slept, tension and fatigue overcoming her. She dozed for perhaps half an hour. When she woke the fingers in hers were cold.

CHAPTER ELEVEN

THE NEXT morning Alex woke up to rain again. Yesterday's sun had cause optimism that the road to Brawton could be repaired within a couple of days, but by the sound of the deluge on the roof such a hope was shortlived. Alex lay and listened to it. The rain suited her mood; the peace of the night had given way to bleakness. Resolutely she pulled back the covers and crossed to her desk. She seized a sheet of notepaper and wrote two harsh lines across it: her resignation.

She found Andrew already in his office. He looked up with quick concern as she entered but before he could speak she handed him the sheet, then stood waiting at the door for his response. When at last he spoke his voice was harsh.

'Coward!'

'I beg your pardon?'

'You heard what I said, Alex.'

Silence. Alex looked at him full on, seeing anger and frustration written on his face.

'I don't know what else I'm supposed to do.' Her voice sounded as if it came from a long way away.

'You can stay here and face up to yourself.' His face sneered at her. 'I'm sorry about Mrs Mac and I'm sorry about the meeting. Margaret told me the outcome—and, before you accuse me of collusion, I was disappointed too. You went about it like a bull at a gate. Now you've had a knock back and Dr Donell doesn't like her lovely plans being rejected. One setback and you're off to a nice safe city job where everything's handed to you on a plate, where you don't get personally involved with your patients and you don't have any nasty Andrew McIntyre breathing down your neck and threatening your precious virginal state.'

'That's unfair!' she protested.

'Is it? Are you going because the board threw out your precious plan, because you lost a friend or because you're afraid of me?'

'I'm not afraid of you.'

'Well, if you're not you ought to be.' He rose and came around the desk. 'I could wring your lovely neck, Alex. You can't do this to the hospital, to me. You come in here and work your way into making the job a success, and as soon as your treasured independence is threatened you quit. What's going to happen at your next job, Alex? Are you going to work in a nunnery?' His hands were on her shoulders, digging in until they hurt.

Alex pushed at his arms, trying to break his hold, but the grip tightened.

'Let me go!' she snapped.

'Why, Alex? Do you really want me to? Is one bad experience going to sour you for the rest of your life?' He looked down at her and his expression hardened. 'What a bloody waste!'

His grip held her hard against him and his mouth found hers. Brutally he kissed her, forcing her mouth open with his lips. She tried to cry out, but the sound didn't come. Pinning her hands behind her head he explored her mouth with his, ignoring her mute resistance. Alex pulled back fiercely, but her strength was no match for his. Her body was pressed against his, hard up against the wall until she felt she could hardly breathe. His hand came up, roughly caressing her breasts, sending shivers of pain and desire through her. She was aware of tears coursing down her face and the warmth of blood on her lip.

Passively she forced herself to go limp under his hands, willing herself not to respond to him. She stayed pinned against the wall, schooling herself to silence and bleak acquiescence.

Her passivity finally broke into his anger. Baffled, Andrew raised his head to look at her. Alex gazed back, steeling herself to meet his gaze coldly, calmly.

'Have you quite finished?' she asked icily.

'Alex . . .'

'Let me go!' She pushed suddenly past him and opened the door. From the safety of the corridor she looked back at him.

'I'll finish at the end of next week. You know the first three months were a trial period on both sides. It hasn't worked out, and you have no hold over me.'

She wheeled around and retreated, diving into the linen store as she heard a nurse approaching. With her luck, she thought, it would be Margaret, and facing the other girl at the moment would be more than she could bear.

In the darkness of the store she stood, shaking and bereft, trying to pull her mind back into some sort of order. She dabbed at her bleeding lip; Andrew had hurt her. She hugged herself, trying to control the sick waves of grief running through her. Dear God, it was like losing Chris and Timmy all over again!

When she had fought herself into a point approaching calm she abandoned her refuge and returned to the flat. There she repaired the morning's ravages as best she could. Her silk blouse was ripped and she fingered her bruised breasts ruefully. Angry red marks outlined where Andrew's fingers had demanded response.

She reapplied her make-up carefully, removing the tell-tale lines of mascara, before making her way to the wards to start the routine of the day.

Janet was just coming on duty, wet and dishevelled. She called a greeting to Alex from the hospital entrance.

'Blithering bandicoots, it's wet out there! It's floods for sure now. The river's still up after the last lot.' She waved a mud-spattered gumboot at Alex. 'Do you like my footgear? All the rage in Pirrengurra this morning.'

'Sister Davis!' Margaret's voice rang out from the office. 'You're an hour and a half late. I want you in my office at once.'

'Yes, Matron. Sorry, Matron.' Janet's voice was unperturbed. 'The points on my car got wet and I had to walk—in this! Talk about devotion to duty!' She hauled the second gumboot off, grinned at Alex and disappeared, dripping, into the office. Alex smiled. She would miss Janet. It was a pity Matron would be the one to tell her about Mrs Mac; the day was bleak enough already.

The hospital was quiet; the day was too awful for any but the really sick to seek attention. The rain showed no sign of easing and by evening the local radio was issuing flood warnings every half-hour. Alex worked mechanically. If she kept busy she could endure the next few days.

Just as the light was fading Janet came to find her. She was finishing afternoon clinic and looked wearily up as Janet came in. Janet's smile had slipped when she had found out about Mrs Mac's death, and now it had disappeared completely.

'What's wrong?' asked Alex.

Janet hesitated.

'We've just been on to Brawton by radio. There's been an accident. One of the trucks slid over the edge—I gather the edge of the road gave way. No one was hurt, but instead of leaving the truck where it was they decided to get it back up on to the road, but with so much heavy machinery and men in one place the whole road slipped and the truck rolled right over. There's a couple of badly injured men and one still trapped under the truck. They can't try and move the truck or the whole hillside will slip. It's looking dreadful.'

Alex straightened up from the tray she had been arranging.

'So now what?'

Janet's face grew more concerned.

'We've been on to company headquarters. They'll get a helicopter up as soon as they can, but it won't be until morning— there's evacuations going on all over the state.'

'So we're going to have to go in,' said Alex.

'Andrew is,' Janet corrected her. 'The road's still out. He's going to have to hike in above the slide.'

'Not by himself he's not.'

'No.' Janet's face puckered and was still. 'Con's going too—we just rang him. He's a local born and bred and knows these mountains like the back of his hand. If anyone can get Andrew across safely it's Con.'

'If there are three badly injured men and all night to go before we can bring them out Andrew's going to have to go prepared to operate. He'll need me,' said Alex.

'I guess.' Janet's voice broke on a sob of fright, then she bit her lip and looked at Alex. For once she had nothing to say.

Alex left her gazing after her. She found Andrew outside the entrance, snapping orders. Already cases were lined up, and Alex recognised emergency resuscitation gear as well as basic surgical equipment. She came to a stop in front of him.

'I'm coming too,' she told him.

Her eyes met his, direct and fearless. He stopped his orders and looked down at her.

'It's dangerous, Alex.'

'You need me.'

He looked at her for a long moment and Alex could see his professional need warring with his personal desire to protect her.

'Move, then.' His tone was abrupt and hard. 'Get some gear on. I hope your feet can cope with those boots by now!'

He yelled the last sentence after her. She had already fled down the corridor to change.

Five minutes later she was seated in the rear of the Land Rover, surrounded by gear. Con was at the wheel with Andrew seated beside him. Janet came to the hospital entrance and stood, a lost look on her face. On impulse Alex leaned out the window.

'Don't worry, Janet, I'll look after them.'

Janet dredged up the ghost of a smile.

'Just don't let them get their feet wet. If they catch a cold we won't hear the end of it for weeks!'

Alex grinned and Con tooted the horn as they swung out of the hospital gates.

Once they left the town Con slowed the vehicle to a crawl. It was crazy to take risks and the driving rain and darkness permitted visibility for only a few feet. Finally, after nearly an hour of painstaking driving, they could go no further. A huge mass of sludge lay across their path.

'How far does the mud extend?' Alex asked.

'About three hundred metres.' Con was already out, adjusting backpacks and checking straps. Can't we just walk across it?'

'I wouldn't like our chances of getting ten metres. The whole lot's sodden and shifting. We have to climb until we find ground that looks like it's going to stay put for a while.' He heaved an enormous pack on to his shoulders, passed a similar one to Andrew and a tiny one to Alex. Alex started to protest, but, as she felt the weight of even her tiny pack, thought better of it. Con handed each of them a large flashlight. 'Let's go. Just keep the noise down, and watch your step. The fewer vibrations these hills have, the better.'

The mountainside had just been logged. Some undergrowth remained, but everywhere huge stumps marked the position of former giant gums. Alex concentrated on her feet, following the beam of flashlight in front of her and conscious of Andrew behind her. The ground was steep and Con went straight up. Alex was breathing deeply after only a few minutes and wondered for how long she could keep up the pace. All the while the steady rain beat down on their faces. Alex thought of Janet's last remark and grinned in spite of herself. Everything she wore seemed to be soaked thirty seconds after she left the Land Rover.

The ground was still churned up after the recent logging. Huge patches of mud caught her unawares and her boots stuck to the ground. A couple of times the mud stopped her dead, but Andrew was there.

'Come on, Alex. You wanted to come on this jaunt. Show us what you're made of!'

Alex flushed and pulled her boot out of the sucking mud, struggling on until she reached the waiting Con. As soon as she neared him he started climbing again, giving her no chance to catch her breath. Her lungs screamed in protest, but grimly she kept going, fighting to keep up with Con's gruelling pace.

Finally they reached the upper limit of the cleared area. Con waited until they were with him and then disappeared into the dark of the bush. Alex took a deep breath and entered the blackness.

The trees were enormous, giants blocking their path at every turn. The undergrowth caught and obstructed their way. Con produced a machete and hacked as he went. Alex fought her way after him, holding a hand to protect her face as branches whipped back at her.

They climbed for perhaps twenty minutes into the bush until Con called a halt.

'I reckon we're a few hundred metres above the worst of the loose stuff now,' he said. 'I think we can go across. We'll have to spread out, though—I don't want us all in the same place at the same time. If you lose us, Alex, don't move and don't call out. Just stand in the one place and flash your torch on and off. Let me get fifteen metres in front and then you start.'

He gave the thumbs-up sign and started across the slope. Alex looked round at Andrew. He put a hand out and briefly touched her cheek, then gave her a slight push. She started after Con, her cheeks burning.

She went slowly, aware that the flashlight in front was also moving cautiously, trying to keep the right amount of distance between herself and Con. Once she lost the flicker of the flashlight in front and felt a surge of panic before Andrew's flash caught her from behind.

'Stop!' His voice was little more than a whisper. 'Flash your light on and off.'

She stood in the gloom, silently clicking the light on and off. It seemed an eternity before Con's light came back towards them. As soon as he knew they saw him he was off again, moving steadily through the undergrowth. Andrew motioned Alex to go on.

Alex made her feet keep going. Her feet squelched as she walked and she threw silent invectives at herself for not getting used to sturdier shoes. Her trousers were soaked from the rim of her jacket down and the wet seeped through her socks downward. Her hood, long since knocked off her hair by a low-hanging branch, hung uselessly behind her jacket and her hair clung to her face. Rain dripped from the huge branches overhead, running down her cheeks and down her neck. Her waterproof gear left a lot to be desired, she decided.

Despite it all, the cold, the discomfort and the pervading danger of another slide, a soft feeling of warmth crept into her. She was on the mountain with two men, one of whom she trusted absolutely and the other whom she loved. She felt Andrew's concern for her in the way his flashlight kept picking up her feet, giving her an extra sureness of step, in his measuring of step to keep pace with her. She thought of Chris in the same circumstances. Chris would have revelled in this night of excitement and danger, but there was no way he would have calmly brought up the rear, checking that she was safe. He would have been out at the front with the machete, hacking his way, leading his followers to safety, and if he lost the odd one on the way—well, they were only followers, after all. She swung round involuntarily and looked back for Andrew. His torch found her face and hers his. For a long moment their eyes held, until she turned back to trudge on. That moment sent a glow of love through her, and her step lightened.

I'm stupid, she thought, but the other little voice in the back of her mind still made her shake her head. She had made her decision. If she left this valley she could be free again.

Free from what? The little voice had no answer. Free from pain? No. The pain was inescapable. To leave the valley was starting to feel like cutting part of herself off. Free from commitment? OK, but what are you if you aren't committed? she thought. Empty? She tripped on a root and abandoned the effort of self-questioning. The ground required concentration. To concentrate on the flashlight in front and the ground below was a feat in itself without thinking about Andrew and her future.

At last Con stopped and signalled them to come up to him.

'According to my calculations we must have crossed the slide now. Well done!' Alex caught his grin in the gloom and turned pink with pleasure.

'We'll start downhill now. Leave off the chat until we hit the road, though.'

He swung away from them and his machete slashed through the barrier ahead.

It was a shock for Alex to discover that going downhill was nearly as hard as going up. Her legs got the shudders and every step she took was an effort. Her stumbles became more frequent and she was aware that Andrew had lessened the distance between himself and her, coming forward to steady her when she needed it.

As they reached the cleared land their pace quickened, but Alex's legs still felt jelly-like beneath her. As they caught in the mud she fought an intense desire to sit down and stay there. Only Andrew's insistent presence behind her drove her on. Her relief as they finally emerged on to the road was indescribable. As her feet felt the solid surface she sank down and put her head between her knees, fighting to stop the waves of dizziness and nausea engulfing her. Andrew bent down and held her head, then as she recovered herself pulled her gently to him.

'Well done, little one! We'll make a mountain woman of you yet!' He kissed her gently on the lips and she didn't pull away.

They rose. Con was standing patiently waiting.

'If you two are quite finished . . .'

They grinned at him.

'Why isn't there a truck here to pick us up?' Alex asked, and then as an awful thought hit her, 'Don't tell me there's another slide further along?'

'No, Alex.' Con's voice was reassuring. 'But we do have a bit more walking to do. The slide is on the edge of a logged area. On the Pirrengurra side the ground is stable right up to the slide, but on this side there's about another five hundred metres of logged area to go before we hit proven stable ground. It'd be stupid to drive a truck in here. They'll be waiting for us at the edge of the cleared stuff.'

The walk along the road was easy. They walked together, with Alex nestled securely in the centre. She felt small, wet and cherished between these huge men. Andrew's hand caught hers and held it. She let it lie. Time enough for confrontation in the light of the morning.

CHAPTER TWELVE

THE DARK and driving rain made it impossible to see their reception committee until they were almost on them. Lanterns loomed out of the darkness, held by men with relief and welcome written plainly on their faces. To Alex they were the most welcome sight she had ever seen. Her legs were leaden, her clothes were sodden and she was shivering uncontrollably. One of the men divested her of her pack and lifted her up into the cab of a truck as if she was made of cotton wool. She sank into the seat, luxuriating in the absence of wind and driving sleet. The truck driver swung himself up and eyed her as if she was some sort of magic being, conjured out of the darkness.

'What's happening?' she asked, and he struggled to find his voice.

'The truck's down an embankment on a side-road just near the camp.' He cast another nervous look at her. 'We'll take you straight there now. We've still got someone pinned underneath.' He bit his lip. 'I dunno, he might be dead by now. We've taken one guy up to the camp, but there's another still near the truck. He looks bad and, to be honest, no one liked to take it on themselves to move him. We've put up a canvas over him and are keeping him warm while we waited and hoped like hell you'd make it.' He eyed her with awe. 'I dunno how you did, though.'

'I dunno either,' Alex admitted. 'With one of those big brutes in front and another behind I guess I was just too scared to stop!'

He grinned and some of the tension eased from his face.

152

'What have you done with Andrew and Con?' Alex asked curiously. 'I only saw one truck.'

The driver's grin increased and he gestured with his thumb to the rear window. Alex swung around and looked through the cab window behind her. Three figures were crouched on the tray. She gasped and then turned resolutely to the front.

'It's times like these I like being a girl,' she confessed.

The side-road when they arrived presented a nightmare scene. At the junction of the main road were several trucks and scores of men, all with the same set look on their faces. Alex climbed reluctantly out of the warmth of the cab and the men on the back jumped down. The camp boss came forward to greet them.

'Thank God! I don't know how you managed it, but I've never been so pleased to see anyone in my life!'

He led them away from the trucks, down the side-road where a floodlight was casting a wavery light through the rain. The road looked as if a giant bite had been taken from it. On the surface was a makeshift tent. A couple of men were bending over a figure immobile under a heap of blankets. Below the road surface Alex could dimly make out the outline of an overturned truck, its wheels pointing upward towards the road. The driving rain pelted over the scene, and even as she watched pieces of the roadside crumbled and fell away. Andrew moved towards the edge and Alex followed, only to be caught and held by Con.

'Nope, Alex. If you'd let us sit in the cab we'd have let you do the death and glory bit, but this is men's work.'

'But——'

'No buts.' His grip tightened.

Andrew stopped at the road edge, looking down to try and make out the figures below. He glanced back at Alex.

'Do your best up here, Alex.'

Their gaze held for a moment, then he swung himself gingerly over the edge of the breaking roadside. The mud and rubble moved with him as he edged tentatively towards the truck. Alex stood rooted to the spot, her eyes never leaving him. She gripped Con's fingers and he also made no move. Andrew climbed inch by inch, the mud oozing and heaving as he did. Alex's breath came out only as he reached the cabin and leaned over whatever it was that lay beneath. She could just make out two other figures, already crouched over the trapped logger.

'How are they going to get him out?' Her voice was a terrified whisper.

Con's voice, when it came, was forced.

'I don't know, love, and that's the truth. That's not your concern, though.'

Alex closed her eyes and fought for control. Her grip on Con's hand must have been hurting him. With an effort she turned away from the edge and retreated to the makeshift tent.

The men crouched over the still figure made way for her. Alex bent over. He was a boy, no more than perhaps eighteen, and it needed little to see that he was critically injured. Almost with relief she realised she was going to have little time to dwell on what was happening to the men near the truck, to Andrew.

Swiftly she began working, setting up a drip, preparing the boy to be moved to somewhere she could work. He had lost vast quantities of blood and was still losing it, she thought, haemorrhaging internally, by the look of it. His injuries suggested he had been crushed by a massive weight as the truck rolled.

He was conscious, moaning softly in pain, and Alex

injected as much pain-killer as she dared before attempting to move him. Finally he was strapped securely to a stretcher and his companions carried him gently up the road to the waiting truck. Alex permitted herself one last despairing glance to the silent party below the level of the road before following her patient.

The truck's headlight flicked on, cutting a yellow swathe through the rain, and the truck moved forward. Alex crouched beside the stretcher, the boy's companions beside her. In the enforced idleness she found enough voice to ask one of the men, 'What was happening back there? What are they going to do?'

'They're trying to hook steel cables on to the truck.' The man spoke in a subdued whisper. 'If the truck moves they'll all go with it. If they can hook on a couple of cables and attach them to something solid above the road at least it'll hold it steady while they try to wedge it up and get him out. It's the weight of the truck that's making the rubble so unstable.'

'Something solid?' Alex turned the plan over in her mind.

'The ground above the road is pretty secure and I reckon there should be a couple of trees that'd do the job.'

'Well, why are they taking so long about it?'

'They need a fair length of cable. They're bringing it down from up on the ridge where we're doing most of our work at the moment. It's a slow trip up there at the best of times.' He paused and looked at her. 'They say he's sweet on you—Doc McIntyre, I mean?' It was a question.

Alex flushed and looked away. The man was silent for a long moment, then he leaned over and put a large hand on her shoulder.

'I reckon they'll be doing their damnedest,' he said quietly.

Alex bit her lip and turned her attention back to her patient.

As they turned into the camp parking area lights sprang on and men appeared from everywhere, eager for news. The figure on the stretcher was carried carefully into the mess hall and laid on a makeshift bed. For the first time Alex could clearly see the extent of the damage, and she didn't like what she saw. She tried to think clearly, but her mind was fuzzy round the edges, refusing to focus on medical practicalities. She settled the boy comfortably, then turned to the man who seemed to be in charge.

'He has severe internal injuries and he's bleeding internally. When can we expect the helicopter?'

'Not till daylight at the earliest, Doc.' The man's face was haggard.

'He has to go before then.' Alex shook her head, trying to clear the mist. 'He won't live until morning.'

The man looked at her for an endless moment.

'There's no way,' he said at last. 'We've put on all the pressure we know and there's just not a 'copter that can get here before then.'

Alex glanced at her watch. One a.m. Another six hours at the earliest and another couple of hours in the air.

The man looked down at the still figure.

'There's got to be something you can do. Can't you operate?'

Alex shook her head.

'I daren't.'

'Why not?'

'Because it's impossible.' Alex's voice was anguished. She stopped and stared down at the floor, minutely scrutinising the puddle her wet clothes were creating on the wooden floorboards. She raised her eyes again.

'There's someone else injured. Where is he?'

The man hesitated, cast another glance at the boy on the stretcher and then shrugged his shoulders. He took her to a corner of the hall where another bed had been made up. A young man lay there, gritting his teeth in pain. His leg had a nasty break. Alex sedated him and let him be. He at least could wait in safety for the helicopter to take him to Hobart.

She was having trouble even deciding that. Increasingly as she worked she was becoming aware of the cold permeating every inch of her body. She couldn't think. She was going to have to do something; in her present state she was no use to anyone.

She turned back to her self-appointed assistant.

'I need some dry clothes,' she told him.

The man looked at her with dismay.

'I'm not after a fashion outfit,' she snapped. 'Just something with a good belt to hold it up, and I'd kill for a dry pair of socks!'

He disappeared, and she sank into a chair with her head on her hands. She closed her eyes and then forced them open as waves of dizziness swept over her. She was still fighting them when her mentor reappeared with a bundle of clothing.

'You choose,' he grinned. 'We found the smallest we could.'

'That'll teach me to be stuck at a logging camp rather than a jockey's convention,' she smiled, and he gestured towards the screens she and Andrew used for their clinics.

She spent an uncomfortable few minutes fighting to remove her sodden clothing. Her knickers were still dry, for which she was profoundly grateful as she surveyed the dubious offerings proffered for her selection. She donned a warm flannel shirt and a pair of loose-fitting trousers with a wide belt. Someone had donated a pair of sheepskin boots, not more than three sizes too large. Alex slipped them on with a sigh of pleasure, then spent a couple of minutes towelling her dripping hair. The bundle didn't stretch to a comb. She pulled the curls roughly back and tied them. Heaven knew what she must look like!

She emerged from the screen to be greeted by a low wolf whistle. She chuckled. Anyone who admired her with her size ten feet had to have rocks in their heads! She flopped as she walked.

It was amazing the difference the dry clothes made. The world seemed brighter and the pale face on the stretcher was no longer a hopeless case. She looked down at him, going over the options in her mind.

'I can't,' she muttered.

'What?' Her assistant was at her side.

'Operate. In these conditions I'd kill him. He might live for a few hours longer, but I'd kill him none the less. If I had another trained doctor here it'd be different.' She bit her lip before continuing. 'But I haven't.'

The man looked at her, his face set.

'Then we just wait for him to die?'

'I didn't say that.' She hesitated. 'You have the company medical records here. Before the loggers come up here they have to undergo a blood test. Can you check the records and see if his blood group is recorded?'

'Hang on.' He disappeared and emerged a few minutes later triumphantly waving a medical form.

'Got it! He's A-positive.'

Alex sent up a silent prayer of thanks.

'Praise be! It's a common group. How are we off for blood donors?'

The man smiled.

'I've got a camp full of men out there, all itching to be woken up.'

'Great. I only want those with A-positive blood, though, and we have to be absolutely sure. I'll need some kitchen staff too. I've got limited sterile equipment, so they can start boiling water. Also,' she put a hand against the boy's clammy skin, 'I want more hot-water bottles. Lukewarm, not hot.' She smiled reassuringly at the man next to her. 'Let's give it our best. If we can't stop the bleeding we're going to have to replace what he's losing, and that's going to take some doing.'

The place leapt into life. Men arrived at the mess hut desperate to be of use. Those with the right blood group were placed in turn on an improvised couch. Others were roped into sterilising, looking after the donors as they finished and filling hot-water bottles.

Alex worked steadily through the longest night she had ever known. One after the other, the loggers came in. The boy in her care stayed alive. Alex watched until her eyes ached, waiting for any sign of deterioration. None came. She moved back and forth from donor to patient until she felt like an automaton. As each new donor came in her eyes swung involuntarily to the door, but there was no sign of Andrew or the trapped logger. She pushed the thought of them out of her mind; she could not afford to allow her attention to wander. Towards morning faint colour started returning to the boy's cheeks and she felt a tiny surge of hope. She felt his pulse. It was definitely stronger.

'How many more donors have we got waiting?' she asked.

'Six.'

Alex leaned back against the makeshift bed.

'I think we might make it.'

'You mean he'll live?'

She shook her head.

'That depends on what they find when they operate in Hobart. At least I think he's going to have that chance.'

They looked at each other, a bond of satisfaction between them.

'Do you think,' Alex's voice was strained, 'you could find out what's happening on the mountain? Surely they should be back by now?'

The man gave a nod and started towards the door. As he reached it the sound of trucks pulling up outside made him hesitate. He looked back at Alex. Alex returned his look blindly and he opened the door.

Voices and shouting came from outside as once more the car park sprang into life. In the faint dawn rays, Alex saw men jump off the back of a truck and reach up to pull a stretcher from the back. Alex started towards the door and met them as they carried the stretcher gently in. She looked down at the face, unconscious against the canvas. It was Andrew.

For a moment her world went black. Her knees gave way under her and she held out a hand, futilely trying to stop herself falling. It was caught. She was held and steadied. The face in front of her blurred and spun as she struggled to bring it into focus. Con. She looked piteously up at him and then down again at Andrew's white face. He was deeply unconscious. His blond hair clung damply to his head. Down one side of his face a huge contusion stood out, bloody and swollen against his ashen skin.

Alex fought for her voice. It came, a tiny whisper from nowhere.

'Dear God!' she whispered.

'Alex,' muttered Con.

'What happened?' She couldn't tear her eyes from Andrew's face. Con's grip didn't lessen.

'We got the bloke out—it took ages. Every time we moved to try and hook the cables the whole lot started shifting. Finally the blokes down there managed to hook them firmly and then they had to dig, shoring the mud up as they went. It was just too dangerous for us to try and help them. They finally got him free. I think he's smashed his hip, but he's otherwise OK. He's on his way here now in the other truck.'

'And then what?'

'We lowered a stretcher and winched him up. The other two blokes down there came up first and Andrew followed the stretcher. It must have been the shifting weight of the three men—the rubble just went. We had the stretcher attached to ropes from the top, but Andrew was carried for fifteen or so metres down the mountain.'

'Dear God!' she whispered.

'Alex, he's only hit his head. I can't find anything else wrong.' Con's voice was almost pleading.

'Yes.'

Her eyes never left Andrew. Her love rose in her throat, overwhelming her, making her feel sick to the stomach.

'Alex, you're going to have to forget it's Andrew.' Con's voice was trying to be firm, but it held a tremor.

'I know.' She closed her eyes. The men holding the stretcher watched her uneasily.

When she opened them she had control. Her voice was tight but efficient.

'Bring him over here.' She gestured to one of the couches. Alex prepared disinfectant and swabbed down the ugly wound. Her fingers probed gently, but there was little to see. Heaven knew what damage there was. There was nothing she could do except keep him dry and warm. She could only wait. She placed a hand gently on his cheek and let it rest there.

'Live, damn you!' she threatened him. Tears welled in her eyes, but she fought them back. With an effort, she gave directions to one of the men to cut away Andrew's wet clothes, then turned away to give her attention to the other man they had just brought in.

Mechanically she prepared a pain-killing injection, soothing and reassuring him as she did. The man was badly shocked and chilled to the marrow. As she helped remove the wet clothes from the injured man she called for hot-water bottles. Every logger in the camp must have relinquished his precious 'hotty' by now.

Before long she had her two latest patients cocooned in a sea of hot-water bottles. The big burner at the end of the hall was stoked to capacity, but still Alex found herself shivering. Perhaps it had little to do with the cold.

The morning dragged on. The men helping Alex looked worriedly at her, and finally Con came forward.

'Alex, you're fit to drop. Can't we take over for an hour or so?'

'You know you can't.' Her eyes were on the drip rate of the young logger. She adjusted it slightly and turned back to him. 'Surely the helicopter can't be far off?'

'I wish I knew.' He was hoarse from exhaustion and worry.

The cook brought her in breakfast, bacon and eggs and a huge mug of scalding coffee. She drank the coffee gratefully but pushed the bacon and eggs away untouched; the sight of the food made her feel ill. Her eyes kept straying to the couch where Andrew lay. he was as still as death in his cocoon of warmth. She crossed to his bedside and took his wrist in her hand. His pulse was weak. I can't lose him too, she thought savagely. The boy with the broken leg called out as the effect of his pain-killers wore off. Gratefully she turned to him. She couldn't allow herself to think past immediate practical need.

The helicopter arrived closer to afternoon than morning. Alex heard it circling overhead and made a silent plea.

'Let it be large. Let it hold a medical team. Let me be able to hand over this responsibility so that I can sit and will Andrew to open his eyes.' She said it over and over to herself as she listened to the sounds of it landing and voices approaching the hut. The camp boss and two other men appeared at the door.

'Are either of you doctors?' She asked the question before the door was closed.

'No.' They looked curiously at her and Alex thought humourlessly of the sight she must present. The first one through the door introduced himself.

'I'm the 'copter pilot and Steve here is a paramedic, an ambulance officer.'

'We asked for a medical team.' Alex knew her voice was sharp, but she couldn't help herself.

'I know.' The man's voice was apologetic. 'There's not one to be had. There's problems all over the state with the floods, and to be honest we didn't see the need. We thought you had two doctors here. It was just a matter of picking one up from Pirrengurra if we needed to take someone to Hobart.'

'They'll all have to go. I can't operate and there are three requiring surgery. I don't know about An . . .Dr McIntyre. I'm going to have to come too. This boy's transfusions can't stop.' Alex gestured towards the boy they had been working on all night. 'How many can you take?'

'It's big.' The pilot was still eyeing her with disbelief. 'It's an Army machine, fitted out to carry injured men. We can fit you all in.'

Alex let her breath out in relief. At least one of her prayers had been answered.

'OK! Let's get going. The sooner this boy is in the operating theatre, the better his chances are.' She didn't add that for all she knew Andrew was slipping away too. There was no way she could tell how serious his head wound was.

The transition to the 'copter went smoothly. The two in charge of the machine knew their stuff and Alex's supervision was minimal. As they loaded Andrew, the last to go in, Con caught Alex and held her back.

'Shall I come too?' he asked.

'To hold my hand?' Her tone was tired and flat. 'No, thanks, Con. I'm a big girl now.'

'Alex?'

'Yes?'

He bent and kissed her, hugging her hard against him.

'Bring him safely back to us.'

'I'll do my best.'

She climbed aboard the helicopter and disappeared from view.

CHAPTER THIRTEEN

ALEX woke up to weak sunshine filtering through the gap in the curtains, leaving a bright strip against her starched white coverlet. For a moment she was confused. She lay against the pillows, soaking in the warmth as she struggled to remember where she was.

She was in hospital. The bed she was in was a hospital bed in a single room, the card above her bed proclaimed her a patient of a Dr Cole. Hobart she thought, and the events of the previous day flooded back. She pushed herself upright, swinging her legs out of bed, only to stop and lie back, confused, as the room started to spin. What was wrong with her? Her legs were screaming their protest at her movement and sharp, stabbing pain was coming from her feet.

The door swung open and a nurse came in bearing a tray. When she saw Alex was awake she smiled, put down the tray and went to pull back the curtains.

'Well, it's nice to see some life in here! Dr Cole said we were to let you sleep, but after fourteen hours I was tempted to give you a poke to see if you were still with us. I decided the smell of coffee might do just as well.'

'Fourteen hours?' echoed Alex. 'What on earth is the time?'

'Eight a.m. You've been asleep since six o'clock last night. Dr Cole said you went to sleep with your head on your arms at his desk in Casualty. You didn't stir when we put you on a trolley and brought you up here. Sister said you helped when she put you into a nightie, but she was sure you weren't awake. Do you remember?'

'No.' Alex shook her head in disbelief.

'Well, it's no wonder, I guess. The story of what you went through is all around the hospital. I love your footwear, by the way.'

The nurse stooped and held up the disreputable pair of sheepskin boots. Alex smiled weakly.

'Now, what about some breakfast?'

Alex looked up at her uncertainly.

'I'm not sure. I just tried to sit up and I felt weird.'

'I'm not surprised.' A voice from the door made them look around. A middle-aged man complete with huge black beard and stethoscope around his neck stood framed in the doorway. 'When did you last eat, young lady?'

Alex shook her head in confusion.

'I don't remember.' Her mind trailed back. Certainly not yesterday. The day before? It seemed like years ago. It was the day she gave Andrew her resignation. She had skipped breakfast and not felt like lunch.

'Not for a couple of days, I guess,' she admitted.

The doctor snorted.

'And you wonder why you feel weird? With the punishment you put your body through it's a wonder you managed to stay upright!'

He moved forward and helped the nurse put Alex into a sitting position, supporting her back with pillows. After a moment the room refocused.

'Now eat, Dr Donell.'

The nurse disappeared. The bearded man stood with his arms folded, watching as Alex ate cereal and two pieces of toast. By the time she reached coffee she was able to pour it herself, her fingers only trembling slightly. She looked up at the doctor.

'I'm sorry,' she apologised. 'I feel a fool.'

'Don't be sorry.' The man's voice was gruff. 'We've been on to Pirrengurra and we know what you've been through. You're going to be sore for quite a while. That hike you undertook was enough to knock you about for a week without the rest on top of it. Your feet are a mess!'

Alex tentatively lifted the covers and peered down at the offending articles.

'Ouch!' she exclaimed.

'Mm. I'll dress them properly afterwards, but if you're up to it I thought you'd probably like a shower first.'

'Thank you.' Alex toyed with the coffee-cup. 'Dr Cole? It is Dr Cole, isn't it?'

'That's me.'

Alex paused. She carefully put the cup down and looked up at him. She couldn't go on.

'They're all still alive, my dear,' he said gently. 'Thanks to you. The two fractures are set and doing beautifully. The lad with the internal injuries is out of theatre and looks as if he'll make it. I dropped in on him a few minutes ago. He was groggy but worrying about who was going to look after his motorbike. It seemed a good sign to me. He owes his life to you, you know. You did a magnificent job.'

Alex flushed and looked down at the empty cup.

'And Dr McIntyre?'

'We don't know.'

Her eyes flew up to his face. The doctor met her gaze directly.

'I'm telling you the truth as I know it. We've done a scan and it's revealed a hairline skull fracture, but as far as we can see there's no other damage. It's just a matter of wait and see.'

'There could be damage the scan wouldn't show,' Alex suggested.

'There could be,' he agreed gravely. 'There's nothing we can do, though, and it's useless to think about what could be wrong.' He took her hand and gave it a squeeze. 'I'm as churned up as you are, my dear, and that's the truth. Andrew and I have been friends for a long time.' He looked at her closely. 'You love him, don't you?'

Alex stared down at the dregs of coffee and said nothing. Dr Cole was silent, his hand still clasping hers.

He straightened.

'He's a very lucky man. I'll tell him when he comes around.'

'If.'

'I said when.'

He turned to the door and then looked back at her.

'Can you cope with a visitor? There's someone here who's been waiting an hour already.'

He stood back as he said it. Behind him, in the corridor, Charlie Taylor's anxious face appeared.

'Charlie!' Alex exclaimed.

Dr Cole disappeared. Charlie came to the door and stopped.

'Can I come in?'

'Oh, Charlie!' Alex burst into tears.

Charlie rose to the occasion with fortitude. He carefully put down the overnight bag he was carrying, came to the bed and allowed her to fling her arms around his rotund frame. He even managed to manoeuvre another of his large red handkerchiefs out of his pocket, though by the time her sobs were reduced to hiccups the front of his shirt was decidedly damp.

'Oh, Charlie!' Alex sniffed and lay back against the pillows. 'I'm so glad to see you!'

'It looks like it,' Charlie retorted.

She gave a watery smile.

'I'm sorry.'

'Think nothing of it, my dear.' He waved his hand grandly. 'Happy to be of service.'

'Oh, Charlie!' she quavered.

He grinned.

'Your record's stuck!'

Alex sniffed again and subsided.

'I'm sorry, I'm a bit overwrought. I guess you remind me of my mum.'

'That's charming!' Charlie's voice was indignant.

Alex giggled.

'You know what I mean. How on earth did you know I was here?'

'Three methods. First, my native intelligence, intuition and sheer animal cunning, second, you're written up in all the papers and third, Janet rang my wife up yesterday with a list of instructions a mile long. By the time I got home from work Elaine had been out buying up Hobart.' He motioned towards the bag.

'You haven't bought me some clothes? Oh Charlie!'

'Will you cut that out? I'll start saying it in a minute.' He bent down and undid the bag. On to the bed came a deep blue woollen skirt with an elasticised waist, a pretty white blouse with a lace collar and a soft sky-blue and white jacket. Alex exclaimed in delight.

'Aren't you clever? They even look my size!'

'Janet gave us all the gory details. Even,' he threw a couple of smaller packages towards Alex, 'down to knickers and stockings. Oh, and shoes.' He produced a pair of light grey leather moccasins. 'Elaine was a bit worried about these, so she bought them a size too big. She thought they'd be better sloppy than tight.'

'Thank heaven for that! I'm going to need loose shoes for quite a while,' Alex explained.

'There's more.' Charlie proceeded to empty the bag on to the bed. Out came a hairbrush, toothbrush, make-up, even a tiny vial of perfume.

Alex picked up the cosmetics wonderingly.

'It's my brand!' she exclaimed.

'As I said, Janet's instructions were explicit.'

'It must have cost you a fortune.'

'Think nothing of it,' he said grandly, then grinned. 'To be honest, my dear, the chairman of the logging company rang me this morning after Janet told him we were doing this. It's all to go on the company slate. It was all I could do to stop Elaine from heading back to the shops.'

'You darlings!' Alex's eyes filled with tears.

'Now don't start again,' Charlie begged. 'You've gone through my only clean handkerchief.'

Alex looked down at the pile on the bed. Half a dozen new white handkerchiefs were tucked among the clothes. She waved one triumphantly and subsided again. Charlie gave her a minute, watching with grave sympathy.

'How else can we help, Alex?' he wanted to know.

Alex blew her nose and leaned back.

'You've done so much. I don't know. I have to see Andrew . . .' Her voice trailed off.

'If you're staying in Hobart for a while will you stay here?'

'I don't know,' she repeated. She looked round her

doubtfully. 'I'm not sick. They'll probably have some other accommodation or I can go to a hotel.'

'Come to us,' he invited. 'Elaine is longing to meet you.'

'It's kind of you,' she said doubtfully, 'but I might be needed here.'

'There's only a certain amount of watching anyone can do, Alex.' Charlie's voice was firm. 'Spend today here and I'll pick you up at six o'clock tonight.'

Alex looked up at him, her eyes still brimming with tears. He put a hand on her shoulder.

'He's a strong young man, Alex. It's going to take more than a hit on the head to kill him. If I were you I'd spend a bit of time on you. If he comes around to that woebegone face he'll think he's dying.' On which cheerful note Charlie disappeared.

Alex gingerly climbed out of bed. Her feet, still tender from the hike of the previous month, had rubbed raw during the long climb through the bush with soaking footwear. She hobbled painfully to the mirror. The face that looked back at her seemed as if it belonged to someone else. Huge black shadows ringed her swollen eyes and her skin was a welter of scratches. She reached up and gingerly pulled a twig from the mass of tangled curls.

Next to her room was a tiny bathroom. Alex forced her feet in there and spent twenty minutes under a cloud of steaming hot water. An hour later when Dr Cole came back to dress her feet she felt almost presentable. The clothes fitted perfectly. She had dried her hair and brushed it until it shone like burnished gold. There was not much she could do about the scratches, but light make-up softened them and lightened the shadows. Dr Cole eyed her with evident approval.

'Wow!' he beamed.

Alex blushed.

He treated her feet with care. Thanks, she suspected, to the dubious sheepskin boots the raw skin had become infected. Dr Cole carefully cleaned them and applied a light dressing. Alex put on stockings. The soft leather moccasins fitted comfortably over the top.

'Ready?' Dr Cole held the door for her and took her arm.

'To see Andrew?'

'To see Andrew.'

He led the way down a short corridor, pushed open another door and stood aside to let her past. As she entered he swung the door closed behind her, leaving her alone.

Alex stood with her back against the closed door, almost afraid to go further. The figure on the bed seemed lifeless. From where she stood there was no sign that he was breathing. His ashen face, made even paler by the stark white dressing on his forehead, merged into the pillow. The thick waves of blond hair seemed dark in comparison.

With fear in her heart Alex approached the bed. She laid a hand tentatively on his chest. The rhythmic rise and fall reassured her.

His eyes were closed. Alex drew her fingers through his hair, gently stroking, but there was no movement.

'Andrew,' she whispered, 'don't leave me.' Her voice choked, but she fought to continue. 'I love you.'

Nothing.

He was lying as he had been placed, his arms rigidly by his sides. Alex put her hand in his and brought it up to her cheek. She sat on the hard chair beside the bed and let her face rest against his chest.

'I'm here,' she said gently. 'I can wait.'

* * *

The days that followed were a blur of misery. Alex spent her days at Andrew's bedside keeping a vigil that became increasingly hopeless. There was no sign of any recovery. She sat watching his face, willing him to open his eyes. She learned every line, every crease, and each time she had to leave him she checked each one for change. Sometimes she held his hand and turned her gaze to the window. Hobart lay below the high hospital building, nestled in the shadow of the towering Mount Wellington. Alex could see the huge bridge, spanning the Derwent and, in the distance, the sea.

'We'll explore it together,' she promised Andrew. 'Wake up and show me this town.'

Occasionally the old nagging doubts would resurface. What she was doing here, binding herself tighter and tighter to a commitment she was afraid of? The doctors and nurses accepted her almost as Andrew's wife. I'm not, she told herself firmly, but I can't leave him like this. I can't.

Each night Charlie took her home. He and Elaine had a comfortable little house, full of memorabilia of a grown-up family. Alex was warmed and comforted by their care, but nothing could help the bleakness of her thoughts.

The chairman of the logging company came into the hospital to find her on the third day. He was visibly upset by Andrew's condition.

'You've both done our company a magnificent service,' he told Alex. 'If there's anything we can do in return you have only to ask.'

Alex smiled, trying to hide her impatience to be back with Andrew.

'Is there any doctor free to go to Pirrengurra?' she queried. She had been having niggles of guilt at the thought of them being without help.

'We've flown in one of the company doctors until either

of you can get back,' he reassured her. 'We've also sent in a helicopter which will stay stationed there until the road is cleared.' He cleared his throat. 'Which actually brings me to the next point.' From his breast pocket he produced a slip of paper and handed it to Alex. She unfolded it. It was the resignation she had given Andrew five days ago.

She sat staring at the words, scrawled in anger and sorrow. Had Andrew posted it off so soon, anxious to be rid of her? Surely not. She looked up at the chairman, a query on her face.

'Matron Nash sent it to me. It arrived this morning.'

Of course—Margaret would have cleared his desk. Alex could imagine her delight when she found this.

The chairman was watching her closely. Gently he took the slip of paper from her fingers.

'Do you want to be held to it?' he asked.

Alex shook her head numbly.

'I don't know.'

'It would be a great shame if you did. The men up there would be bitterly disappointed. Since this happened our headquarters have had one phone call after another from our men out there, practically ordering us to look after you.'

Alex smiled, but the worried look stayed on her face.

'I phoned the hospital after I received this,' the chairman went on. 'Matron Nash was out and I had a very long and informative chat with Sister Davis.'

'Janet?' queried Alex in surprise.

'That's right. She gave me three reasons why you might be leaving, two of which I might be able to do something about.' He sat back and looked at her. Alex said nothing and waited for him to continue.

'Sister Davis took the opportunity to let me know she was

resigning her full-time position. She wants half-time work after she's married. She seems to think driving by yourself up to the camps was a strain and the clinics at the camps were too much work for a doctor alone. She offered to accept a job twice a week assisting with Andrew's clinic at Kinley and twice a week with your clinic at Brawton. That's four half-days. She did have a suggestion as to how she could fill in the other half-day.'

'I'll bet!' Alex grinned in spite of herself.

'Well, since word got around the camps of your moves to get a health centre, the women have been up in arms about it. It seems you've tapped something which they feel they need. In view of their pressure and the pressure to look after you, we're prepared to fund it. We'll run it for a trial of three months and if it's used we'll continue indefinitely. That's two of the items on Sister Davis's list.' He hesitated. 'The other I can't do a thing about. I can only hope you can sort it out between you.'

'If we get a chance.' Alex was almost speaking to herself and the chairman had to bend forward to hear.

'As you say.' He rose. 'Can I put this away for a while to give you time to think about it?'

Alex nodded mutely.

He tucked the piece of paper back in his pocket, looked at her for a long moment, then departed down the corridor. Alex went back to the silent Andrew.

By the fifth day Alex was starting to lose her sense of perspective. She was having trouble sleeping, no matter how comfortable Charlie and Elaine made her, and she was jumpy and on edge. Towards evening she was gazing out of the window of Andrew's room at the arc of lights across the Tasman bridge when Dr Cole came in. She didn't hear him enter and when he touched her arm she started and burst into tears. He looked at her, troubled.

'You've had enough, Alex, and that's the truth. I don't want to see you in here tomorrow.'

'Of course I'm coming in.'

'Nope.' He shook his head resolutely. 'You can pop in tomorrow evening for half an hour, but for the rest of the time this room is out of bounds to visitors. That's you.'

Alex turned to him, distressed.

'I know—it seems cruel. You, however, are still my patient and you're not doing yourself any good at all. You have to have a break.'

Charlie and Elaine when they heard were in full agreement.

'Why don't you take my car and do some sightseeing?' Charlie suggested. 'Go down to Port Arthur for the day.'

'Port Arthur?' she queried.

'It's an old convict settlement an easy drive from here. It's a beautiful place. Would you like us to come with you?'

'No, thanks.' Alex tried not to sound as uninterested as she felt. The last thing she felt like doing was wandering round being a tourist.

The next day, though, as she left Hobart's boundaries and headed along the coast road, she was forced to concede they might be right. Already her head felt clearer and her mind sharper. A parcel of clothes had arrived from Janet, so she was wearing her own jeans and a big colourful sweater. She turned the radio on in Charlie's little car and concentrated on the scenery and the music. The country was lovely, winding roads, closely settled farmlets, and hills rolling in all directions.

She slowed down as she crossed the narrow neck of road

leading into Port Arthur. The place was bleak, eerie and beautiful. The stone ruins stood harsh against the vivid green countryside and the steel grey of a wild sea.

There was a guide, taking a small group on a tour of the ruins, but Alex was content to wander on her own. The wind was biting. She could taste the sea.

She settled on a rock outcrop, facing out to sea. For the first time in a week she was completely alone, her mind free to wander where it might.

She thought of Chris and for the first time since he died she could think of him without pain. There were some good times, she thought, and found she could remember them without bitterness. She thought of the times of their marriage and found herself smiling at stupid, funny things she had forgotten, things that had been pushed away in the overriding hurt of his neglect. I loved you, Chris, she said softly to herself, and found herself thinking of him as one might a child, almost as she did of Timmy. She had loved them both.

And have I the courage to start again? she asked herself. The tiny voices were at last stilled. She loved Andrew, not the adoring hero-worship she had once felt for Chris but a strong, deep love that wanted to serve and share forever. She knew Andrew felt the same. She had rejected his gift of love. She could only hang desperately to the hope that she would be given another chance.

She closed her eyes, listening to the wind screaming around the desolate ruins. I'll come back in summer, she thought, and see you at your best. By the time she rose stiffly and made her way back to the car she felt as if the ruins were her friends. Perhaps it's the ghosts of the convicts with all their tales of misery,she thought, telling me to grab my chances. She smiled, but the image stayed with her.

She drove slowly back to Hobart, feeling strangely at peace with herself. Just outside the city she stopped at a roadhouse and had a light meal. She sat alone, watching the darkness fall and the lights of the night appear. After her second cup of coffee she paid her bill and slowly negotiated the unfamiliar streets until she was back at the hospital.

The nurses on duty greeted her as a familiar friend when she appeared. For a moment she felt the oppression of the day before descending and fought to keep her feeling of peace. She opened the door of Andrew's room and a pair of calm blue eyes looked at her.

She walked towards him, her eyes not leaving his face, scarcely able to breathe. The eyes crinkled into a tired smile. His hand moved on the coverlet and Alex reached forward. Strong fingers closed around hers. He whispered her name and she bent closer, her heart alight with joy. The huge, oppressive burden of worry lifted.

'You're mine,' he said.

CHAPTER FOURTEEN

FOR Alex it had been a long, tiring afternoon. The work had banked up while both she and Andrew were away. The young relieving doctor had been able to do little more than the urgent work; the routine work, the check-ups, injections, house calls and paperwork had fallen to one side.

Alex returned to Pirrengurra as soon as she was sure Andrew was safe. There seemed no logical reason why she should stay in Hobart. The harsh truth that it tore her in two to leave him seemed irrelevant to the rest of the world.

He hadn't asked her to stay. Since those first precious moments when he opened his eyes they had lapsed into an odd formality. Alex found the tiny hospital room claustrophobic. It closed her in, robbing her of the ability to say what she so desperately needed him to hear.

Andrew, in return, was content that she was there. He slept as would a man who had been deprived of sleep for months, hours of deep, untroubled sleep, moments of wakefulness and sleep again. In those moments of consciousness his hand searched for hers, his fingers slowly stroked hers until the effort became too much and he slept again. In those quiet times Alex fell more deeply in love than she had ever dreamed she could be. Her heart, her life was in his keeping and her whole being sang a song of joyfulness and peace. And yet when the pressures mounted and she had to return to Pirrengurra he made no demur. She gently kissed him goodbye and left him sleeping.

That had been a fortnight ago. When she returned the work

engulfed her. She worked ceaselessly, determined that Andrew should come home to a clean slate. Sometimes she rang the hospital in Hobart to check his progress. Sometimes, as the patients came in one after another and she thought she would never come to the end of it, she asked Janet or even Margaret to ring for her.

She and Margaret had achieved a truce. When Alex had arrived back Margaret had been mortified. Neither mentioned the letter of resignation and, as Alex put her head down and worked, Margaret seemed to come to some sort of acceptance. They had reached the stage where they worked together efficiently and their respect for each other grew. Margaret would never be a close friend, Alex thought, but without the conflict over Andrew they could achieve a kind of rapport.

The letter of resignation still lay in the keeping of the logging company chairman. One part of Alex told her she should ring and withdraw it, another told her she should wait. She ached to see Andrew again, but mixed with the ache was fear. She was exposed, she knew. Her heart was wide open. Oh, God, if he didn't want her! In the sanity of daylight, as she immersed herself in work, she had faith in him. She knew that he was hers and she put all her being into working for him. In the dark corners of the night when the hospital was still and dead she lay awake, overtired and imagining.

Perhaps it was a game. Perhaps when she was wholly his she would be rejected. She desperately needed to see him, to feel his arms holding her against him. The reports from Hobart said 'recovering slowly'. The wait was dreadful.

Part of her wanted to run as far from Andrew and this hospital as she could. She was trapped, held by the fine gossamer threads of her love for him, waiting for whatever he willed.

She finished clearing the surgery and switched off the lights. As she came out into the hospital corridor the sound of a vehicle pulling into the hospital entrance and the voices of the nurses as they emerged to open the doors made her grimace. More work! She rounded the corner and looked down the gleaming length of linoleum. There at the hospital door, surrounded by welcoming staff, was Andrew.

Alex pulled back. She couldn't bear to greet him like this, surrounded by people. Her fears rose up and washed over her, leaving her cold and shaking. She stood with her back to the corridor, listening to the welcoming laughter and talk. His voice rose above the others, clear and resonant.

'Where's Alex?'

She couldn't face him. She whisked away into the sanctuary of her flat. I'm being stupid, she thought. I have to face him sooner or later. Later, her cowardly mind answered. She grabbed a coat and headed out of the french windows, down the long embankment to the river.

The calm of the night greeted her like a friend. Two wallabies, already out, raised their heads in vague resentment before resuming their nibbling. The moon was up, casting a silver glow over the shimmering grass. There was going to be a frost.

Alex made her way down the path, feeling her way in the dark. Halfway down a rocky ledge jutted over the river. Alex stopped and sat, curling her coat around her. Below her the creek was still a river. It hurled along in frenzy, rushing the masses of water dumped on the mountains in the past few weeks down to the plains. The moonlight sent ripples of light over its foaming path. The noise of the water was a background to the soft rustling of the trees overhead and the tiny noises of small night creatures out on their forage for food. Alex sat listening. What was it Mrs Mac had said? All it takes is courage.

How long she stayed there she couldn't tell. The peace and beauty of the place seeped into her, soothing her fears. Her mind, caught in the turmoil of the last few days, settled and calmed. She caught again the feeling she had among the ruins of the convict settlement at Port Arthur. She was sure.

She rose stiffly. The moon was high in the sky. The two cheeky wallabies on the lawn below the hospital had been joined by half a dozen of their mates. Less sure of her, they leaped for the safety of the bush at her approach. She pushed open the door of her flat. Andrew was sitting in the dark, in the big armchair beside the gas fire. Only the flicker of the gas flames showed that anyone was there at all.

'Been bushwalking again, Alex?' His voice was a mixture of amusement and tenderness. Alex felt her heart leap. She was suddenly shy.

'You've got me addicted,' she told him.

'How are the feet?'

Alex grinned.

'If they're not tough now they never will be!'

He rose and came towards her. In a sudden gesture of defence she flicked the light on, and winced in the harshness of the light.

He looked well. A dressing still covered his forehead, but his tan seemed deeper, highlighting the blond of his hair. The creases around his eyes were deeply etched, reacting now to the glare of the light. He wore trousers and a big Aran sweater. Alex found herself mesmerised by the fair hairs showing above the V of his open-neck shirt and blushed, forcing herself to look away.

Andrew was doing his own perusal. He caught her and swung her around to the fire.

'You're freezing! And tired. Your eyes are like black saucers. What on earth have you been doing to yourself?' he demanded.

'Missing you.' The words were a whisper, but they echoed around into the far corners of the room.

Andrew sighed, a long-drawn-out sigh of happiness and relief.

'Oh, my love!'

He caught her to him and held her, as one might hold a child who was hurt or frightened. His face settled in her hair.

They stayed locked, neither wishing to break the spell of happiness hovering over them. Alex's cheek nestled into the thick folds of his sweater and stayed there. Here was her home.

Andrew was the first to break the spell. His hands caught hers and held them.

'You really are freezing, little one. How long were you outside?'

'I'm not sure,' Alex admitted.

'Why did you run?'

She searched his face. What she saw reassured her.

'I was afraid,' she confessed.

'Of me?'

She shook her head.

'Perhaps. Not any more.'

He gave a low, triumphant laugh.

'I'll bet you haven't eaten either, Alex Donell.' He pushed her away from him. 'You're to stand for ten minutes under hot water while I try my hand at an omelette.'

She protested weakly, but he pushed her firmly into the

bathroom and closed the door.

She had to admit the hot water was heaven. When she finally emerged she was glowing pink. Ruefully she realised she hadn't brought a robe into the bathroom. She looked at her pile of clothes. They were damp and cold. Nervously she tucked a white, fluffy towel around herself and headed to the door.

On the low table before the fire Andrew had two plates, each bearing a magnificent yellow omelette. Knives and forks, her crisp white linen serviettes and glasses of wine completed the picture. Alex took one look and dived for the bedroom door to find her robe, only to be caught and held by the laughing Andrew.

'No need, my love. You look magnificent the way you are, and this flat is nearly as warm as you.'

'But I'm not respectable,' she protested weakly.

'Aren't you?' He held her at arm's length, considering. His gaze raked her long, slender legs, upward to her thighs, glowing with the heat from the shower. Slowly he continued his inspection, to her breasts standing proudly erect under the flimsy covering of the towel to her blushing face. 'No,' he agreed solemnly, 'I don't believe you are.' He swept her up in his arms and deposited her unceremoniously on the rug in front of the fire.

His omelettes were mouth-watering. Alex ate with hunger, savouring each mouthful. Her glance kept flicking up at him, always to find him watching. She blushed and concentrated on the omelette for a little while, then her eyes would creep back to him. He had pulled his sweater off. His shirt front lay open and Alex felt an overwhelming desire to run her fingers through the golden hairs on his chest. He caught her eyes and laughed at her, and her blushes deepened.

The meal ended. Andrew refilled their wine glasses and pushed the low table out from between them. He raised his glass in a toast.

'Here's to us, my lovely Alex, my own sweet love.'

Alex looked at him for a long moment and silently raised her glass. She took a sip before the glass was lifted from her clasp and she was taken into his arms.

She melted into him. His hand came up and loosened the knot at the back of her head, letting loose a cascade of chestnut curls. His hand rippled through the mass. With a groan he sank backwards on to the rug, pulling her after him. She lay on his chest, looking up at him. He put a finger on her mouth, tracing the course of her lips.

'I've asked you before, little one. Will you marry me? Will we live together, have children together, grow old together?' His arms encircled her, holding her down against him. 'Can you start again?'

'Oh, Andrew!'

She drew her face up to meet his. His mouth enveloped hers, his tongue searching, pushing into the recesses behind her lips. She placed her hands down on his chest, drawing apart the soft cotton of his shirt. Her fingers moved gently through the waves of hair on his chest, marvelling at his maleness. With an aching sigh he left his careful stroking of her hair. The soft folds of the bathtowel were pulled away, leaving him free to run his fingers along the satin-smooth skin of her thighs, around along the flatness of her stomach and up to cup the soft flesh of her breasts. He pulled her upwards, his mouth caressing each nipple in turn until Alex cried out in ecstasy. She pushed her hands beneath his head and pulled him upright until she was seated on his knees, her legs straddling his thighs. Her hands moved softly, exploring the hidden places behind his ears, caressing the soft hollow of his neck, feeling the strength of the muscles in his back.

Suddenly their need was more urgent. Andrew moved to loosen his own clothing as a knock echoed through the flat. Alex gasped and moved backward, reaching for the safety of her towel, but before her hand could locate it Janet walked into the flat.

She came perhaps three paces into the room before her eyes registered what was happening. She stopped, her eyes wide with dismay.

'Whoops!' She appeared rooted to the spot. Her face filled with a mixture of amazement and delight and her eyes started to crease into laughter.

Alex was speechless. She looked down at her nakedness and back at Janet, then fled into the sanctuary of her bedroom. She slammed the door and stood behind it, trying to decide whether to laugh or cry.

Andrew remained his calm, unruffled self. He rose, lifted Janet up bodily and deposited her back on the hospital side of the door.

'Much as we love you, Janet, your presence is just a trifle out of place at the moment.' He slammed the door on her laughing face and strode back into the bedroom. When are you going to get a lock on that blasted door?' Alex couldn't reply. She was doubled up, tears of laughter streaming down her face.

'It's all right for you, Dr Donell, but I've got my reputation to consider. You haven't got a choice now.' Andrew lifted her into his arms and glared into her laughing face. 'We're going to have to get married. Alex Donell, for the third and last time, will you marry me? Do you dare to love again?'

'Oh, yes,' Alex breathed as he deposited her on the bed.

The last of his clothing disappeared and his body gently lowered into hers. The night dissipated into a shower of stars. Their bodies merged into a glory of love, allowing no room for fears or doubts or heartache. 'Yes, please!'

GIFT OF GOLD *Jayne Ann Krentz* £3.50

One dark night in Mexico, Verity Ames tantalized a knight in shining armour – Jonas Quarrel. To release himself from a tormenting nightmare, he was compelled to track her down and discover all her secrets…

A WILD WIND *Evelyn A. Crowe* £2.99

Ten years ago, Shannon Reed and Ash Bartlet had planned to marry, but disaster struck. Now they have been given a second chance, until Shannon is accused of murder…

SHARE MY TOMORROW *Connie Bennett* £2.75

It was a dream come true for marine biologist, Lillian Lockwood – not only working with the renowned submarine pilot, Neal Grant, but finding such happiness together. But only by confronting his ghosts could Neal bury the memories which were crippling their love.

These three new titles will be out in bookshops from April 1990

W❂RLDWIDE

Available from Boots, Martins, John Menzies, W.H. Smith, Woolworths and other paperback stockists.

Mills & Boon

HELP US TO GET TO KNOW YOU

and help yourself to "Passionate Enemy" by Patricia Wilson

Patricia Wilson's classic Romance isn't available in the shops but can be yours FREE when you complete and post the simple questionnaire overleaf

Mills & Boon

ROMANCE
Passionate Enemy
PATRICIA WILSON

FREE

Romance Survey

If you could spare a minute to answer a few simple questions about your romantic fiction reading, we'll send you in return a FREE copy of "Passionate Enemy" by Patricia Wilson.

The information you provide will help us to get to know you better, and give you more of what you want from your romance reading.

Don't forget to fill in your name and address – so we know where to send your FREE book!

SEE OVER

Just answer these simple questions for your FREE book

1 Who is your
 favourite author? _____

2 The last romance you read
 (apart from this one) was? _____

3 How many Mills & Boon Romances
 have you bought in the last 6 months? _____

4 How did you first hear about Mills & Boon? *(Tick one)*
 ❑ Friend ❑ Television ❑ Magazines or newspapers
 ❑ Saw them in the shops ❑ Received a mailing
 ❑ other *(please describe)* _____

5 Where did you get this book?
 _____

6 Which age
 group are you in? ❑ Under 24 ❑ 25-34 ❑ 35-44
 ❑ 45-54 ❑ 55-64 ❑ Over 65

7 After you read your
 Mills & Boon novels, ❑ Lend them to friends
 what do you do with them? ❑ Other*(Please describe)*
 ❑ Keep them ❑ Give them away _____

8 What do you like about Mills & Boon Romances?
 _____

9 Are you a Mills & Boon subscriber? ❑ Yes ❑ No

Fill in your name and address, put this page in an envelope
and post TODAY to: Mills & Boon Reader Survey,
FREEPOST, P.O. Box 236, Croydon, Surrey. CR9 9EL

NO STAMP NEEDED

Name (Mrs. / Miss. / Ms. / Mr.) _____

Address _____
_____

_____ Postcode _____

You may be mailed with offers
as a result of this questionnaire

PWQ1